A Ghost for Christmas

CROWVUS

First Published in 2020

Crowvus, 53 Argyle Square, Wick, KW1 5AJ

Copyright © Cover Image Crowvus 2020

ISBN: 978-1-913182-22-9

www.crowvus.com

Foreword

It is always one of the highlights of the Crowvus year when we can share our Christmas ghost story book with you all. This year, we are offering you a treasure trove of ghost stories: ones which will terrify you, others which will make you smile and cry at the same time.

This has been a very tricky year for everyone. For some people, it has been a more than tricky year: it has been a painful or horrible year. Most people will be pleased to put it behind them. But it is a year when we have needed creativity and imagination more than we ever have done before.

This year, we had more entries than ever, with an outstandingly high standard overall. Thankfully, we had already enlisted another judge, so we had an extra pair of eyes to help us make the difficult decisions of who to longlist, shortlist and place.

But really, the competition is only one tiny part of the book. The main part is you, the readers. Each and every one of these writers has created a doorway for you to open, walk through, and explore what's on the other side while you get a reprieve from the stresses of 2020.

Enjoy!

Archie

by Teresa Bassett

(1ˢᵗ Place)

Jane met Archie in late November. A year to the day since the death of her husband.

Although she'd never considered herself sentimental about dates and anniversaries, it had hit her hard. She found herself staring through the window as she washed the morning dishes, remembering how Geoff loved that view of the woodland. Minutes went by as she stood, quite motionless, tears cooling on her cheeks.

The day was frosty and still, and Jane decided a brisk walk might shake off the melancholy. She strode along the sunken green lane behind the pub, a solitary figure in winter coat and boots. At the end, in no mood to return home, she took the footpath cutting up through the stubbly fields, empty now of the sentry-like corn which had flourished in the summer.

Before cancer had bent him double, she and Geoff loved to explore the countryside around here, particularly the old church beyond the rows of yews and skeletal oaks. She'd avoided going there without him—it seemed wrong somehow. Today, by contrast, Jane felt oddly drawn to the place, as though something compelled her to take a look.

Shadowed by the trees, she inched along a path overgrown with bracken and bramble.

She squeezed through the gate, which stood rotting on its hinges. The church itself had long since fallen into decay, and only a couple of tumbledown granite walls remained. Fragments of slate from the roof littered the ground. The air smelled of damp leaves, and the yews seemed to watch silently, unstirred by the slightest ruffle of breeze.

Ascending three stone steps, a noise made her pause, instantly alert. Quiet sobbing, coming from behind the tallest wall. This place was so remote, Jane shouldn't investigate alone, but no way could she ignore those plaintive cries. She crept further, ignoring the quickening in her chest, the tingling at the nape of her neck. The sound grew louder. It wasn't sobbing—she could tell that now. More like the whimper of an animal.

Behind the moss-covered wall, a dog stood tied to a pillar. Fur totally black, ears pointed like a fox's. Secured by a string threaded through a tatty collar. A dirty plastic bowl lay overturned, just out of reach.

The dog stopped whimpering and raised sad, droopy eyes. The thin tail gave a slight movement, as though the dog wanted to greet her, but was too dejected or weak to give a full wag.

Jane's surprise turned to anger. Who could leave a dog in this isolated place? How long had the poor thing been here? From the skinny ribs showing through matted black fur, it might have been days.

She moved forward slowly, holding out her hand. "It's all right," she whispered.

The dog remained motionless, staring into her eyes. Didn't seem afraid, just exhausted, and glad to see a soul. She bent down and the dog sniffed her fingers. She stroked its neck, hot to the touch. Then she noticed a scrap of paper tucked into the collar. She tugged it out, unfolded it and read the spidery message.

Please look after Archie. Things have taken a bad turn for me. Can't look after him anymore.

Jane frowned, then dropped to her knees beside the dog and gave him a gentle hug. He leaned into her, quivering slightly.

"Hello, Archie."

Jane untied the string and walked the dog home with her. He moved slowly, panting with the effort. Every now and then he paused to catch his breath, holding her gaze as though anxious she'd go on without him.

Inside the warm cottage, the first thing she did was put down a bowl of water. Archie lapped it up, licking the bowl dry. Next, she made a round of pilchard sandwiches and put one, broken into pieces, on a plate in front of him. Archie stared, then sniffed, and in a moment the food was gone. Jane felt encouraged. It had to be a good sign that he could eat and drink. While he ate, he seemed visibly to gain in strength, which led Jane to offer another fish.

Although she'd always loved dogs, Jane had never had one of her own, partly due to Geoff's allergy to fur, partly to their love of travel, not wanting to be tied down. Strange how things change, she thought. Nowadays she had so few ties, she feared she might float away, and there'd be no one to pull her back.

She ought to contact a local animal shelter, or even try to track down the owner, who sounded in need of help. But even as she thought it, she realized how difficult that would be. She hated the thought of Archie being reunited with someone who clearly couldn't cope with him. Worse still, she'd heard terrible stories of people claiming dogs who weren't theirs, in order to sell them.

Archie didn't look like an expensive pedigree, definitely a crossbreed, she'd have said, but all the same …

Archie crouched and watched her, paws outstretched, tail gently beating the floor. The look in his brown eyes was clearly one of adoration. It wouldn't hurt to keep him for a while, would it? While she worked out what to do?

*

By the time Christmas came round, all thoughts of finding Archie a home had vanished from Jane's mind. His paws were well and truly under the table, and she wondered how she'd ever managed without him. He kept her fit, forcing her out for walks in all weathers. Best of all he loved her in the selfless, unconditional way of dogs, which few humans have mastered.

She'd had him checked by the vet and he'd been declared under-nourished, but essentially sound. He flourished under her care, and the gentle tail jerks of the first day were soon replaced by thumping great wags of approval, and barks of delight whenever Jane arrived home from a trip out. The only concern Jane had was a curious expression that came into his eyes occasionally. A worried look, maybe wistful, as though something played on his mind.

On Christmas Eve, for the first time since Geoff had died, Jane made preparations for a Yuletide feast for herself and Archie. Nothing too fattening—she didn't want to ruin Archie's new-found health, but there was a free-range chicken to share, and he'd also be having carrots and peas, a roast potato or two.

Despite being spoiled rotten all day, Archie wasn't himself. Instead of curling up beside Jane on the sofa to snooze after his walk, he paced the lounge, restless, looking round at her and letting out a faint whine. Jane hoped he wasn't ill. He seemed fine otherwise, so she decided to see how things went. If he was the same by the end of the holidays, she'd take him to the vets.

During the night, Jane awoke from a troubled sleep. Certain she'd heard something downstairs, coming from the kitchen, where Archie liked to sleep. Heart racing, she remained still and listened, eyes wide in the dark.

There it was again. Scratching. She must stay calm. Archie needed to go out, that was all. She scolded herself for being a fool, sensing danger in every creak and rustle. Usually Archie slept right through, but there were bound to be exceptions.

As she slipped out of bed, the scraping sounded again, and this time she heard a muffled whimper, too.

She hastened down to the kitchen and switched on the lamp. Archie stood by the back door, scratching at the wood, whining. He turned and stared, then renewed his clawing.

"You want to go out?" Jane felt puzzled by his unaccustomed behaviour, the alert expression in his eyes.

The moment she opened the door, Archie bolted down the path and disappeared among the shrubs at the bottom of the garden. Jane stood in the doorway, shivering, scanning the frosty grass. Normally, Archie ambled quietly around the lawn and borders, never venturing beyond the bushes. Where was he headed with such a sense of purpose?

No breath of wind stirred the silence. Jane waited, her skin prickling. There was a gap in the hedge beyond that dense foliage, and she'd been meaning to block it off for some time. Since Archie hated to be parted from her for even half an hour, it hadn't been a problem until now.

Jane grabbed a coat from the door hook, slipped her bare feet into cold shoes and hurried along the path. Pulling the coat close, she forced her way between berberis and holly, fighting a growing sense of dread. The thought of losing Archie now was unbearable.

Beyond the shrubs, she glanced left into darkness, then turned right, moving between more large shrubs. She stopped, her breath catching in her throat.

Archie stood in a clearing by the hedge, a few paces ahead. There was someone with him, crouched at his side, arms around his neck. She opened her mouth to cry out, alarmed in case the stranger meant him harm. It was immediately clear, however, from their stillness, the way they leaned together, that Archie wasn't distressed.

The man didn't appear to have heard her. He knelt in shadow, but a sliver of moon revealed his face, upturned to the sky. A young, bearded face, lean and pale.

Jane stepped back, unsure what to do. She must intervene in case this man wanted to make off with Archie, but she also realized how unwise it was to accost a stranger in the middle of the night. He might have a knife on him, or worse.

Her love for Archie gave her courage. She backtracked quietly for a few steps, then moved forward again, rustling branches and calling Archie's name. Rounding the bushes, she found the two still embracing.

Archie turned his head and twitched his tail. The man looked at her. The moon vanished behind clouds, casting his face into shadow.

"He's yours, isn't he?" Jane said dully.

He shook his head. "No, you belong to each other. I gave up that right when I chose the next fix, the next bottle."

"The bad turn," Jane said, remembering the note in Archie's collar. *Things have taken a bad turn for me.*

He nodded.

"So you don't want to take him?" Jane cursed herself for even asking. There was no way she'd give Archie up without a fight.

"Don't worry." The man—scarcely more than a boy—smiled. "I had to make sure he'd found a good home, that's all." He tousled Archie's fur and dropped a kiss onto his head. "I was so out of things when I left him, I don't even remember where it was. I just hoped to God someone would come. Someone like you."

Jane sighed. "Come inside. You look cold. Are you hungry? Come and have something to eat."

"No, I'm going now. I just wanted to see, to make sure."

"Things are better for you now?" Jane asked, reluctant to let him go.

"Oh, yes. Much."

He released Archie, who, tail wagging, ran up to Jane. She hugged him and told him what a good boy he was. By the time she raised her head, the stranger had gone. Only then did she wonder how he'd found them.

*

Jane spent the rest of the night on the sofa, unwilling to be parted from Archie for even a second. On Christmas Day, they feasted on chicken with all the trimmings. She thanked Providence that she had him with her, safe and sound. She asked herself if she ought to do something about the man she'd found at the bottom of her garden, but had no idea what. That evening, curled up with Archie, his head in her lap, she picked up a local newspaper she'd been meaning to read for several days. Leafing through, her gaze fell on a photo.

She gasped. The photo showed the man she'd seen, she was sure of it. There was no mistaking that thin, bearded face, those haunted eyes. The article alongside concerned homelessness. People were having to be turned away from overflowing hostels, it said, even at Christmas, even in a countryside area like this.

Her heart pounded as she studied the photo again. The young man had been found on a remote lane, dead from an overdose.

"But that can't be right," Jane said aloud. The newspaper was dated mid-December, and the boy was said to have died in November.

She looked at Archie, who watched her with soft, devoted eyes. All day he'd seemed puffed up with joy, as though something had been settled in his mind.

"It can't be …" said Jane, half to herself. There must be some mistake. Some explanation. She remembered the young man's unearthly pallor. She remembered his words. *I had to make sure he'd found a good home.*

Had he come back, somehow, to check up on the dog he'd let down so badly? Archie thumped his tail, and Jane went to fetch his lead.

A Living Nightmare

by Eleanor Harvey

(Children's Winner 11-16 years)

You wake up suddenly. You must have been roused by some noise from outside; a fox, perhaps, howling through the dark. Not that you can imagine there is much dark allowed to exist under the harsh streetlights of your road.

But then you remember. You're not in your road now; you're in a hotel in the Peak District. That's why the sheets look so white even in the darkness, and why the fabric is so smooth and unlike your own bed, which is covered with a homemade patchwork yellow and red blanket, a present from your daughter-in-law.

Strangely, you don't feel tired, just uncomfortable. You usually like staying in hotels because the beds are so comfortable, as this one had been when you first climbed into it; but now the sheets feel scratchy, clinging to your limbs as if trying to restrain you.

Don't be silly, you tell yourself. Just turn your quilt over to the cool side and you'll feel refreshed. You take your own advice, but it makes the situation worse, not better.

Now the bedding is too cool, weighing down on you like the cold metal of chains. You sit up, reaching for the light switch. After all, everything gets scarier when it's dark and you are telling yourself to go to sleep. You brush your hand against the leather of the bedstead, and then move towards the bedside table where the lamp sits, but you can't find the switch. You sigh; the air is heavy and oppressive, but it is one of those air-conditioned rooms with sealed windows, so you can't even get up and let in some fresh air. You get up anyway. It is unlikely that you're going to get back to sleep after all this fuss, so you stand up and walk towards the window. You draw the curtains open, admitting some light from the floodlit car park. You turn away, deciding to go for a short walk to calm yourself down. The air in the room is still thick and uncomfortable, whilst the vague silhouettes of the furniture seem threatening in the weak illumination coming from outside. You'll just get dressed and go outside for a minute, then come back and go to sleep.

Five minutes later, you're outside in the car park, looking up at your room on the third floor. Your curtains are blowing about in the cold wind that's breezing through the trees which are dotted around the rows of vehicles surrounding you.

There is just one problem: you can't open the windows in your room.

The Ghost of Christmas

by Isla Burns

(Children's Winner – under 11 years)

Once upon a time there was a spooky ghost who took all the lights, Christmas trees and presents. In the morning a little girl called Isla found out that there was a large storm in the middle of the night. It was a week before Christmas and I was so excited I could burst.

On Monday I was getting ready for school and I saw something in the shadow then it disappeared.

I asked Mum, "Mum, when are we going?" and she said "once you're done."

When I was at school my friend asked me, "did you hear that noise?"

"Yes," I said, "it was sort of a screeching noise, wasn't it?"

"Yes it was," my friend said.

My sister was at school, her name is Holly and she is a good sister!

When I got home my brother asked me, "did you hear the storm last night?"

"Yes, I did," I said.

"What, what's that? Oh no, we've got to tell Mum, but what is it? It's a ghost!"

"We've got to hide!" shouted mum.

Next door was the mayor, so we went to their house. He had a ghost gun which captured ghosts.

Boom!

"We got rid of it!" I cried. "Can we go back home to have Christmas?"

"Of course," said Mum.

Miss Corrie's Children

by Karen McDonald

When it came to recounts of strange goings on or notions of the supernatural, I had always tended to follow the sceptical fraternity. Believing that there was always clear, sound logical reasoning behind everything. I am a man of science after all.

It was February, midterm break couldn't come quick enough and I'd long had a hankering to visit Uig on Lewis. Not an obvious choice, the Outer Hebrides are wild and unforgiving at that time of year, battered by storms off the Atlantic. But exactly the kind of remote escape necessitated by my more challenging, unruly students.

A spell of browsing had turned up a perfect gem, Tigharry Schoolhouse. Perched above a pristine beach with views to Harris, the blurb mentioned it was thought to be haunted by the ghosts of former pupils. Well, I was amused by such a ridiculous idea and undeterred, though the irony wasn't lost on me. I was packed and on my way before sunrise the day after school broke up.

The road northwest gives way to ever more stunning scenery, the highlight without doubt, the breathtakingly beautiful Glen Torridan. Its towering mountain range was catching the winter sun through tumbling clouds, revealing spectacular snow drenched summits. I got out with the dog to stretch the legs and though my toes nipped and the sharp cold air burnt my lungs I wished I could have lingered there longer. The once daily ferry from Ullapool left the mainland and took us over the choppy Minch waters to the Isle, and from the port it was nearly an hour to Uig.

 When I arrived, the sun had already dipped over the ocean. In the midst of all the shadowy blue that shrouded the uplands of this unfamiliar landscape, the warm glow through the pub windows was a welcome sight. Entering the low cottage door the modest bar room was thick with the smell of peat smoke. The landlord kept the keys for Tigharry and was expecting me. I took a seat at a table by the fire's hearth and supped a half pint while he rustled up some fish and chips. Ollie was stretched head to tail on the flagstones at my feet. The locals were friendly and I guessed spent as much time in the pub as at home. I too, was reluctant to leave its warmth. Somehow it always feels a little like being an intruder when you arrive at a strange place to stay, especially after dark. So reluctant was I, that when offered a whisky nightcap - on the house – I obliged, even though I can't bear the stuff. I was encouraged by my bar mates, they have a mite more relaxed attitude to drink driving laws at the far reaches of the islands. In any case, I could see the schoolhouse not more than a few hundred yards away. Which was lucky, since the full tumbler suggested they don't bother with measures either.

My key rattled open the heavy schoolhouse door into a porch. I hung my belongings on the shaker pegs and roamed from room to room, turning on the lights. The old scullery, toilets and storerooms provided the bathroom and two very sparsely furnished bedrooms. A narrow hall displayed black and white photographs of the school and its former occupants dating back to the mid-1800s. This opened out into a large double-height living area that would have been the classroom. First impressions were good, its whitewashed tongue and groove walls, mid-century furniture and reclaimed timber floors looked every bit as charming as the website had promised and the central heating was a God send. Honestly, after the long day travelling and a belly of whisky I got into bed, dog curled at the foot and was out like a light.

The sun still hadn't appeared over the hill when Ollie's barking woke me. I got up, forgetting where I was for a second and went down the hall. It was icy cold. At first I thought the heating had switched off through the night, but a door ajar at the back which I'd thought to be locked was the culprit. Ollie was outside barking at the swings, I figured he'd forced the handle to get out and shouted him in. A couple of logs in the wood burner and some hot coffee later, all was well again and fair weather was forecast for my day ahead. But my mind kept returning to my arrival the previous night, trying to retrace every step and remember if I'd checked the back-door lock. The wooden sash windows bore glimpses of the rugged Harris hills to the south horizon and to the stunning beach below Tigharry. With the sun now bathing the crescent shore I pulled on boots and jacket and grabbed my camera.

Ollie raced off down the well-worn trail as if he'd run it a hundred times. Near the bottom the craggy hill path gives way to tufted, long grass and rabbit holed mounds before opening out onto the sweeping, white sand. We walked its length and clambered out over the rocky pools at the north end. There was a warmth in the sun felt more keenly in the shelter of the bay and the salt sprayed air was heavy with the scent of fresh kelp and fish. I felt like I could be a million miles from anywhere, castaway and alone. Perfect.

We'd been out for hours, I was calling Ollie back up the beach when I saw a woman on the cliff top near the schoolhouse. She looked quite striking, her long red hair flowing behind her in the breeze. I laboured up the steep embankment, Ollie energetically bounding up ahead. She remained for a time until I next looked up from my feet and she was gone. Once at the top I scanned the area but there was no sign of her.

Now I can't explain it, but back inside I suddenly felt very uncomfortable. Acutely conscious of all my movements and of the noise they were making, even the sound of my own breathing. I felt like the intruder again. Like I'd stumbled into someone's house at an awkward time uninvited. I knew this was completely irrational but it didn't stop my heart from racing, until I could hear it and feel it pounding in my chest. Ollie too seemed unsettled, always by my side. I put on some music to fill the silence and re-set myself.

Mercifully, after what seemed an eternity, it was close to dinner time and I hastened out the door and up the hill in the gloaming to the pub.

I felt relief inside its thick stone walls. Like a walker up the hills, grateful for a bothy to 'coorie doon' out of a storm. The landlord greeted me warmly and I took a seat at the empty bar. He poured a straight up dram of whisky and set it down. I'd not asked for it, but I needed it. I took it in one swift gulp and ordered a pint and 'the special' for dinner. I knew what I wanted to ask him, but when I heard the words in my head they sounded absurd.

When he returned from the kitchen I came out with it, I asked if there was anything to the claim that the schoolhouse was haunted. He laughed, shaking his head, "nothing but a few bored bairns at a caper," he said.

I joined Ollie by the crackling fire, frankly comforted by the landlords' dismissal. I'd no sooner started my dinner when a voice said, "It's real." I turned over my shoulder to see a frail old gent hunched over a whisky in the dimly lit corner, gnarled fingers as black as coal. His name was Alexander Gair, folks knew him as Sandy and he'd lived there all his life. That night he told me all about Tigharry School, where he'd attended as a boy before joining his father on the boat. History records that in 1856, a deadly influenza swept through Uig and the island at large. It cut short the lives of many children and elders, including those of Tigharry. Sandy claimed he and many who'd lived near the school had heard children of a night when the school was in darkness and empty. One janitor is said to have quit his post and left the area overnight leaving nothing but a note of apology. The school was closed for good a few years later, a dwindling school roll the justification. I brought over a whisky for Sandy though he was still nursing the first. I never saw him touch a drop all night, but I was surely glad of one for what he told me next. He spoke of a woman from the mainland who holidayed at the old school. A primary teacher, no children of her own. She lived to be a teacher and found the school holidays lonely. Sandy believed she found solace in the spirits of the children that haunted Tigharry and returned time and time again for many years. Her name was Jean Corrie. The story goes that she met and fell in love with a young man from the area and was finally happy before tragedy struck. Nobody knows to this day how she fell to her death, but her body was found at the foot of the cliff by Tigharry Schoolhouse. Sandy claimed her spirit remained there still, haunting the old school with the children.

I bid him and the landlord goodnight and, steeling myself, returned to my lodgings. The wind had strengthened, the swings out back swayed and creaked and loose slates rattled on the roof. A draft whistled under the old door, I built up the fire, slumped into the chair by its heat and fell asleep.

It was near 1am when I woke to see Ollie stood rigid at the window - his hackles raised, growling and barking fiercely. It was wide open and the drapes were billowing in the rushing cold air. I jumped up to slide it closed and through the glass I saw her. It was the woman with the red hair. She stood - perfectly still, staring out to the ocean. I jumped, sure that I heard the pitter-patter of feet down the hall. It was then I realised the place was in darkness and flicked on the lights again. When I went back to the window she was gone. I quietly opened the door and stepped out. I called to see if anyone was there but no reply came. I went back inside, locked the door and checked all the windows. My body was shaking, partly from the bracing cold but undoubtedly because I had possibly just seen the ghost of Jean Corrie. The nerves swelling in my gut surely believed it.

I told myself whisky didn't agree with me and put the kettle on. I stoked the dying fire embers and fed them with tinder and kindling and pulled Ollie close. I'd decided I'd not be taking to my bed down the hall and was settling in for a long night when I spotted an old book on the floor. Perhaps the wind gusting through the open window had toppled it from its resting place. But if you asked me, I'd swear I'd seen no such book there before.

I opened the hard-bound cover at the beaten corner. The yellowed page inside revealed its contents. It read, "Journal belonging to Miss Jean Corrie." My stomach turned but with some trepidation I continued reading its penned pages. Every creak of the walls and rattle of the roof stole my attention, but fuelled by adrenaline and strong coffee I pored over every page. There was one entry I'll never forget, the last one.

Sept 23rd, 1928

Time has passed slowly without my love here. The school no longer offers me comfort, instead the beach has become my constant companion. I'm counting the days till the boat gets in, our marriage can be blessed and Sandy can carry me home, the new Mrs J. Gair.

No, I thought. It can't be. I picked up my phone and started researching furiously and it wasn't long before I found it. Death records show she died two days later, September 25th. Recorded as a fatal accident. She had no known next of kin. Community news covered the event, expressing sympathy for their own Sandy Gair, who would have been wed to Miss Corrie that coming Saturday. Below that was a further link for Alexander Gair. I clicked on it and my heart stopped when it opened. Alexander, (Sandy) Gair had died at home in Tigharry, October 1st, 1989 at age eighty-six, over twenty years before my visit and our encounter in the pub. He'd never married and had no children. Impossible, right?

I left the journal on the windowsill, packed my bag and left a day early later that morning. The landlord waved from behind the bar, "Come back and visit us soon, George," he cried. I smiled and nodded as I got in my car but I knew I'd never be back, fearing if I did – like Miss Corrie, I might never leave.

The experience thrust open a door between the known and the unknown and shook me to the core. I've been of a mind ever since that there are more forces at work in this world than science.

The Message

by I. M. Merckel

Christmas Eve, 1995, Canon City, Colorado.

There was no snow, despite the snap in the air, not unusual for our high desert town at 5,300 feet elevation. I wouldn't have noticed anyway, for as a child approaching my sixth birthday, I was overwhelmed by my discovery.

"Mom, Dad, I see Santa," I shouted. "His sleigh and reindeer too."

How I must have looked, small of stature, face aglow, as I stood there clad in my Roy Rogers cowboy pyjamas. My friends had seen Santa in the Department Stores, but as far as I knew no one had viewed him flying with his reindeers and sleigh.

"I see him, Jeremy," my mother said softly, following my finger directed at the flickering light in the night sky. Squinting, I'd made out the movement of the reindeers' legs at full gallop, followed by the sleigh, and in it the figure I knew had to be the jolly gift deliverer. He was coming to my house.

"Me too," my father joined in.

"Let's tell Teresa. It'll make her feel better. I told her Santa would come."

"Shhhh, Jeremy, let her sleep," my mother said. "She needs her strength so she'll be better tomorrow when we see what Santa brought. We need to go to bed now so he can get here."

I didn't protest, more from self-interest than a desire to obey, for I feared disobedience might bring a last minute adjustment to the delivery of items contained on my "being good holiday toy list." Yet, falling asleep at that moment had as much chance as an appearance in our front yard of my favorite cowboy and his horse Trigger. How could slumber arrive after what I'd discovered?

Periodically I arose, quietly tiptoed to the front window, and re-confirmed my sighting. Each time Santa seemed closer. During my fourth trip, while slinking by my parent's bedroom, I heard them talking, my father saying, "Let him believe what he saw was true. He's only five."

"I know. But shouldn't we prepare him? The doctors say it could happen any time. They can't do anything more. At least she's home in her own bed. They're so close to each other, almost like twins. They seem to know what the other's thinking. You saw the Christmas card he made for her."

"The drawing of the tree and ornaments on the front. The message inside."

"'Get better so we can have Christmas together always.' When he made me write that I almost broke down. Now, seeing Santa in that star. The sweetness, the innocence, the love our little boy has."

"Let's wait a little longer — make this the Christmas he'll remember. He's got the rest of his life to figure out there's no Santa Claus."

My father was right in that it was the Christmas I remembered, but not for the reason he'd hoped. I was awoken not by the clatter of reindeer hooves on the roof, but from the stomping of feet, the commotion in my sister's room, the garble of radioed messages, my mother's sobbing, and my father telling me people were helping my sister. His assurance made little difference, for all I thought about was her leaving, and those words from behind the bedroom door, that "there was no Santa Claus."

*

My mother's family had lived in Canon City for generations. They owned a large family plot in the Resurrection Cemetery, where most of our ancestors lay. Teresa rested there now, her spot marked with a small headstone. She had been eight.

The family tradition was to place in the casket personal items to accompany the departed. My contribution was that card I'd made for her, the only one I'd ever done. I kept for myself a snapshot of the two of us, Teresa with her long golden hair spilling out from a silly party hat, smiling her wonderful smile, her arm around me, while I blew out my five birthday candles. I slept with that photo under my pillow until the images faded.

Following the service my father handed me Teresa's favourite stuffed toy, a small teddy bear. "Your sister asked that you keep it safe for her." I thought it should have gone into the casket, but since she wanted it for me, I took it. It was placed in a box with other remembrances of her — of our times together.

*

Christmas Eve, 2019, Canon City, Colorado

"We hope you'll join us tomorrow. We do a nice Christmas breakfast. Why don't you come this year?"

Henry Gilsup was the portly, white haired, middle-aged Sheriff of Fremont County, Colorado. I'd served him for seven years and was now his Senior Deputy. Our County covered a lot of territory, but few towns, a fact I liked, for doing patrol allowed me the isolation I appreciated. I used the solitude, if the mood struck, to talk to Teresa. You'd think someone at six feet, with strong Nordic features, a face many thought pleasing, a steady law enforcement job, would have his life together after twenty-five years following a tragedy. That hadn't happened for I still missed her deeply.

"Thanks for the invitation, but I don't do Christmas. Santa Claus isn't my thing. I'm going to the cabin, read some books, and veg out."

"If I'm not mistaken, you've got no family here, and no significant other. You'll be alone. That's not right"

"I am alone. My parents and sister are gone. I'm used to that. I relax, enjoy the quiet, commune with nature. I appreciate the extra days off you've given me."

"Your parents died young?"

"Not so young. I was born in their late forties. Both passed in their sixties."

"We start at 9:00 and go 'til noon. If you change your mind, the door is open."

"If I were you I'd keep the door closed. We've got a storm coming. Could get snow."

"That makes Christmas better."

"Merry Christmas, Henry."

*

My shift ended at two. My first Christmas Eve stop was always the cemetery to place pine wreaths on the graves and have a talk with my sister. She now rested between my parents, a vacant spot beside her when it became my time.

"I miss you, sis. Hope mom and dad are with you, wherever you are. Work's fine. I'm okay. I got invites for tomorrow but you know that's not for me. Tonight's the night I feel we're closest. I wish I could have done something for you, but there weren't many options for a five-year-old wannabe cowboy. At least you're at peace. I'm glad for what we had."

You need to move on Jeremy. What's done is done; what is, is. I'm fine. Get on with your life. Don't stay in the past, embrace the future. Live the life you're given. You know I want that for you. I'm always with you.

That was the answer I usually heard. It was my head repeating the well-intended clichés my friends provided. Saying them was easy. Accepting them wasn't. Maybe I just need more time.

*

My cabin sat fifty feet off the backway to the San Isabel National Forest. It wasn't much of a road by then, just single lane chip and seal. Most travelled the four-lane highway and then back-tracked to the area on the county road, but that took longer. Besides, I enjoyed the quiet of the rural drive and was usually the only one on it. My closest neighbour was three miles away.

The snow started as I left town, and got heavier as I rose in altitude. It didn't feel like a major storm, but when I arrived at my cabin there was a five-inch accumulation, with big soft flakes continuing to fall, coating the ground and surrounding pines in pure white. In the late afternoon the world resembled a Currier and Ives Christmas scene.

My retreat had two rooms and a bath. The main room was a combination living/dining/kitchen set-up, furnished with a small dinette set, couch, cushioned recliner, and a television on a T.V.

stand, all inherited from my parents. The best part was the stone fireplace whose fires could warm the room. The mantel above it held family pictures in dated frames.

Next came a small bedroom with a double bed, nightstand and dresser, also inherited, and adjacent to that my bathroom with a sink, toilet and tub. A propane generator provided electric to run the lights, appliances, septic tank, and space heaters when needed. My indoor water system drew from a well. Behind the cabin was the shed I used to store things my small in-town apartment had no space for, things I couldn't bring myself to dispose of.

The set-up was rustic, fine for me; an idyllic retreat in which to spend a snowy day — and to forget.

The sun set mid-afternoon at this altitude, three days following the winter solstice. I'd just put logs in the fireplace, my intention being to settle into the recliner in front of a warming blaze, leaving the unpacking for later, when the wind began to howl — hard and mournful. Then, a knock at the door. Never before had I received a visitor. Not knowing what to expect, I cautiously opened it to find a small girl, perhaps seven or eight, standing in the now swirling snow. Bundled in a stocking hat, muffler, snow outfit, and rubber boots, all in red, her cute face, small nose, pretty mouth and dimpled chin were all rosy from the cold. Her eyes were her most notable feature — big, dark, and wide-open — reminding me of the works by Margaret Keane. My sister had loved pictures of those large-eyed children.

I looked beyond her, but saw no one. When I returned my gaze she was staring at me. "How did you get here? Where are your folks?" I said softly, trying not to frighten her.

The urchin was silent, eyes locked on mine. I checked again, but saw no one. I brought her in, out of the gusting wind, and to keep the snow and cold out. Removing her muffler and coat, she followed me to the fireplace where I started the fire. My desire to go through her garments for information was deferred, for I needed her to trust me first.

As the fire warmed, she removed her ski cap. Shoulder length dark hair cascaded, framing her now pale skin and those glorious eyes. As it tumbled I pretended to sneeze. Her face contorted into what appeared to be a giggle, but there was no sound. Well, at least I got her to show some emotion.

"That's better. What's your name?" Again, no answer.

Her outfit was spotless. She smelled of cinnamon, spice and gingerbread. In that condition she couldn't have been out in the woods long. Curious.

As she watched the fire, I called dispatch, speaking loudly over the raging wind, and asked for reports on a missing child, or accidents in my area. There were none. Explaining what I'd found — actually what found me — they promised information would be sent as received. I provided her description and advised that with the weather conditions, she would spend the night here, to be brought down on Christmas. I was now entertaining a holiday visitor.

*

Dinner was finished — tomato soup and grilled cheese sandwiches, as only a bachelor could ruin them. Despite the sub-standard fare, she ate most of her serving, watching me all the time. To my questions she remained mum, just staring. But things changed when I pulled out some marshmallows, for she walked over to the fireplace, the fire now blazing, and waited. At least she's familiar with toasting marshmallows.

After our "dessert," I took her to the bathroom, located my spare toothbrush, still in the wrapper, the way it came from my dentist, and my tube of toothpaste, suggesting she brush. I pointed to a washrag and soap, and then went in search of nightclothes for her. When I returned, having selected my spare pyjama shirt as the only likely covering, the toothbrush was in the holder, her face shone from washing, and the washrag sat folded on the side of the sink. She knows how to clean herself, and has good manners.

"Would you like to take a bath?" No response. Had she appeared dirty, or not smelled so sweet, I might have forced the issue, but felt no need to do so. I gave her the pyjama shirt with instructions to change and then went to make her bed. Then, a thought. "I'm going to the shed for a minute. I'll be right back."

Into my coat and hat, for the temperature had dropped significantly, I grabbed a flashlight and trekked through the fierce wind and blowing snow to the shed, thinking this must be what it's like in the Himalayas. It took me a few minutes, moving things around, before finding the box containing my sister's effects. Hurrying back to the warm cabin, I found my now barefoot guest in front of the fireplace, staring into the flames, dressed in my red and green checked pyjama shirt that hung down to her ankles.

"How'd you like to read Christmas stories?"

A small smile was her response.

"Okay." I pushed the recliner closer to the fireplace, added another log, and pulled out the child's version of 'A Christmas Carol,' one of Teresa's favourites. "You know, it'd be a shame to only have the two of us enjoy this book. How about we invite a friend?"

She looked confused, glancing about the cabin, seeing no one else present. Her eyes returned to me, questioning. I smiled, reached into the box, and pulled out the teddy bear received after the funeral. Her eyes got bigger, as if that were possible, and she held out her arms.

I sat at one edge of the recliner; she squeezed in beside me, the bear in her lap. The story told the familiar tale of Ebenezer Scrooge, but in a much shorter, watered down, less frightening manner. The ghosts were more fairy-god-mother type characters, akin to Cinderella's.

"When I was young, my sister used to read this book to me. She liked doing that."

No answer.

As I read, my guest scrutinized the illustrations, and when done, her tiny hand would turn the page and I would continue. At times I stopped reading, thinking she'd fallen asleep, but after a pause she'd look up at me, so I resumed. The crackling fire and the howling wind created a perfect backdrop for the reading.

When I finished, she sighed, and stood up in front of me, bear in hand.

"You liked the story?"

She smiled.

"Can you tell me your name?"

She walked over to the hearth. Wrong question.

When she yawned I suggested it was bedtime, for it was close to 9:30. Her response was to look at the box that had housed the book and teddy bear.

"You win. I'll read one more Christmas story, but after that you need to go to bed. We have a lot of things to do tomorrow so you'll need your sleep."

She walked into the bedroom while I returned to the box for the other book my sister loved — 'A Visit from St. Nicholas,' by Clement Clarke Moore. It also contained bright depictions that, along with the poem, had kept Teresa entranced.

The child lay in bed, propped up by the over-sized pillow, the bear lying beside her. Her clothes were neatly folded on the chair in the far corner of the room. "Since you won't tell me your name, I need to name you. I think I'll call you 'Merry', as in Merry Christmas. Is that all right with you?" I received a smile.

"This was my sister's favourite book. She read this to me all the time, even in summer." Knowing I wouldn't receive a response, I lay beside her and began. When I finished and started to close the book she stopped me, re-opening it to the beginning, and then placed her small hand on mine, awaiting a second reading.

The touch staggered me; its lightness overpowering. So innocent. Within that small cabin — amidst the blowing snow and moaning winds, the crackling fire, and smell of the pines — my heart jumped, my eyes teared, my soul opened, and my thoughts went back to those happy holidays before that long ago night. The shackles that had attached to me a quarter of a century before, seemed lighter. My voice wavered as I read, pausing at times to regain composure, all brought on by that elfin paw still resting on mine. After finishing, our hands remained together a few moments, then she rolled on her side, next to teddy, and closed those wondrous eyes. In a minute, her breathing told me she was asleep. I leaned over and kissed her soft cheek.

"Goodnight, Merry. Pleasant dreams."

I quietly went to her folded clothes, seeking information. I found nothing. In the process I suddenly felt I was being watched. I turned but the child's eyes were closed, her breathing steady. I better wait until morning to see if she'll give me some information.

*

Christmas Day, 2019

I awoke in the recliner, back in its usual place, in the cold main room — no heat. I was still dressed in my uniform. The only light was provided by reflected moon glow off the snow, seeping in around corners of the shaded windows. Checking my watch's luminous dial, there remained several hours before dawn. The winds had stopped, the storm apparently had moved on.

In the gloom and quiet my grocery bags sat on the dinette table, unpacked. The fireplace held stacked logs, but no evidence of a fire. I tiptoed to the bedroom. The bed had not been used. In the bathroom, flipping the light switch, I found my spare toothbrush, still in its wrapper, no washcloth on the side of the sink. All the cabin windows were fastened; the cabin door's inside bolt was thrown. There was no way she could have left without leaving open her means of exit. I called dispatch to confirm yesterday's call-in. There was no record. My sister's box of possessions was missing.

Grabbing a flashlight, I stumbled to the shed through six inches of snow in the pre-dawn still. The box was buried underneath others — dusty, sealed with aged tape. A walk around the cabin disclosed only my footprints.

Were Merry's beautiful eyes, her sweet smile, her holiday scent, the touch of her hand, the warming of my heart, the sharing of what had meant so much to my sister and I, mere illusions? Was I dealing with another holiday disappointment? If it had been a dream, what was its purpose? People hallucinated; some unfortunately remained mired in them. But not me. I didn't believe in fantasy. I was too practical, finding explanations for confusing moments. But this had me stymied.

Then, on the mantel, I found a sprig of pine.

Changing my clothes, I returned the supplies to my vehicle, and shut down the cabin. My attention was diverted to navigating the treacherous snow-covered road, amidst the dark, now silent pines which lined my path, as I descended to the city. Yet, my mind churned with thoughts, hopes, and questions.

*

The cemetery was deserted that still Christmas morning. The storm had largely spared the city, leaving only an inch of snow on the ground. In the bitter cold, the only sound was the crunch of the snow underfoot, as I followed the path trodden countless times before, marked by the grey impassive slabs identifying the final resting places of so many. It could have made a nice backdrop for a Halloween movie, but this was not about treats, costumes, or ghouls. There were questions afoot, and a Sheriff's Deputy who required answers.

I always approached the family plots slowly, for I felt I was performing an act of reverence for my ancestors. Inconsistent as that may sound coming from a realist, I believed my deliberate approach honoured their lives. It was a sacred rite I adhered to.

A faint glow of dawn began to lighten the sky in the east as I approached my sister's plot. Not a bright change, more a shifting from black to dark grey, but it provided enough light to stop me in my tracks, for my eyes focused on a small bundle resting against my sister's headstone. Blinking, shaking my head, I took several more tremulous steps, as the object became clearer. The nearer I got, the more overwhelmed I became, for there was no question as to what I saw. Years of disbelief, scepticism, and denial, based on suppressed anger caused by an event over which I had no control, evaporated, replaced by an indescribable uplifting of spirit. There before me, atop the snow, against her headstone, was my folded red and green pyjama top, and sticking out from its folds was a Christmas card, the only one I had ever made — given to my sister those many years before.

With trembling hands, a pounding heart, tears running down my face, I sank to my knees, opening the card in that thin light, and found several long strands of hair which I knew had to be of the golden colour I remembered so well.

I cried, laughed, then jumped, shouted, and turned about, all in celebration of a new understanding, for I now realized that those words I'd heard in my head all those years, comments I believed were mere echoes from others, emanated from the soul of my long departed sibling. Gone, yes, but still here. The connection had been there all along, I was just not open enough to receive it. Yet, the appearance of a small lass (a messenger?) set the stage for acceptance.

"I get it. I hear you now," I shouted with joy. In exultation, I turned to my father's grave. "Sorry, Dad. You were wrong. That Christmas is not the one I'll always remember — this one is." This awakening was the most wondrous gift of all.

I looked up at the sky, beginning to lighten, but not enough to hide the stars. And there it was, in the spot in the heavens where I knew it would be, that flickering light. I squinted and made out the reindeer, the sleigh, and the hefty gift giver, just as I had those many years before.

Standing alone, as the morning light came, I revelled in my discovery. I wanted to remain, but it was time to leave, for there was a Christmas breakfast to go to now, a holiday to celebrate on this first day of my new understanding. Under the now brightening skies I shouted out what I hadn't uttered in decades. "Merry Christmas to all." And for the first time since I was five, I meant it.

Salt Dough Stars

by Lorraine Thomson

The loft has a distinctive odour she finds hard to define. Thinking that perhaps it comes from the insulation, she sniffs close and gets a whiff of not very much. The roof is sound, no tang of damp. The space does not smell fusty or mildewy. No hint of slime, it's dry and dustless, not even a cobweb, though there's always the feeling that something is scuttling beyond the feeble circle of light thrown out by the single bulb.

Twice a year she comes up here, once in January to return the boxes to their place and again in December to bring them down. Each time, she tells herself to replace the bulb with one much brighter. One with a brilliant glow that will eradicate the dark corners, but she always forgets and perhaps that is just as well for what would the creatures that lurk in the shadows do if she deprived them of their habitat? Thoughts of what might be skulking in the edges send a shiver through her. She hears Jim's voice echo in her head, *someone walk over your grave*? She tuts, the expression one she has never liked.

Despite there being no evidence of anything living here, her mind fills with images of creatures she loathes. Scuttling spiders, scurrying rats, flitting bats, fluttering moths. She shudders. Why must she torment herself this way? She's always been the same. When she was a child and car sick, her mind immediately conjured visions of onions frying in a thick, bubbling gloss of oil, her stomach curdling as her nose filled with an aroma that was not there.

One other thing she does not like about the loft is how cramped it feels. This is because of the low ceiling. She can only stand upright in the dead centre of the apex, where the roof crowds to a point. Moving around, she must stoop and take care not to bang her head against the rafters. The stooping and hunching make her feel claustrophobic. As soon as she's up here, she wants out again.

Despite the lack of damp and dust, the boxes are coated in a film that has built up over the year. She wants to wash her hands as soon as she touches them. She should have worn gloves. She's had these thoughts before, has them every time she's up here. Lightbulb, spiders, rats, bats, moths, hands, gloves. The thing to do is find somewhere else to store the boxes and then she will never have to come up here again, but first she must take them down. One by one, she carries them to the side of the loft hatch where she will be able to reach them while standing on the ladder. Each has a list of its contents taped neatly to the side.

BAUBLES & TINSEL, the baubles a confusion of colour nestling between layers of coiled sparkle. She's never been one for themed decorations, her tree festooned each year with a mishmash of shiny globes reflecting the joy of Christmases past.

Inside TREE DECORATIONS salt dough stars, long ago brought home from nursery by the girls, are daubed with silver paint and patches of flaking glitter. There are Nutcracker soldiers, flying geese, ceramic candy canes, silver cherubs and a host of other trinkets, home-made, bought, and gifted, each wrapped in tissue and memories. Her daughters are grown now, but they still come home for Christmas, bringing bottles of wine and partners and friends. They tease her about the tat and glitz, but if she leaves as much as a broken-nosed Santa out of the display, complaints arise. Her tradition has become their tradition. It is part of their love.

In this box labelled ORNAMENTS nestles the Nativity scene with the one-eared donkey, the other lost before it could be glued back on. The wide shallow box marked TABLEWARE holds the red and gold placemats, the Santa gravy boat, the once-a-year turkey platter. There are boxes containing candle holders and candle arches, decorative felt stockings, red and green and trimmed with tartan ribbon, an inflatable Rudolf, and last year's cards to be used as this year's gift tags. Finally, there is a plain brown carton, unfamiliar and with no list taped to the side. She frowns then shrugs and places it beside the rest. Perhaps it contains a few odd bits from last year. It will be exciting to find out, but first comes the tricky part of balancing each box between herself and the ladder as she descends rung by awkward rung. She takes a moment now, as she always does, to stare through the hatch at the section of hall she can see below, this making her feel as though she is peering into her home from another world, except she can't see the hall for the hatch is closed, the ladder folded neatly into the loft. Something flutters against her cheek. She brushes it away telling herself there is nothing up here.

The hatch is closed but there is no-one in the house. Tricky though it is by herself, bringing down the decorations is a task she has long since claimed as her own. She always does it when Jim's out so there is no interference, no helpful suggestions, everything done just so. The light, 40 watts of dim, flickers. Her gaze is drawn to the plain brown carton with no list on the side. She kneels and peels away the tape holding down the flaps and opens the box. On top is a layer of crushed brown paper. She removes this, revealing a vase which she takes out and examines. It is delicate, made of thin, white porcelain. She has never seen it before. She removes the next layer of crushed paper and finds a set of unfamiliar figurines. She wonders who they belong to and what they are doing here. She looks around and sees more boxes stashed along the length of the loft. She crawls to the nearest and opens it. There are photo albums inside containing pictures of people she does not know. The next box holds paperwork, old bills, official correspondence. The names on these she does not recognise but the address elicits a gasp. Her address – their address – with the names of strangers attached. The word *no* escapes her lips, the sound a long, low ache that she feels rather than hears. The light flickers again, as though in response, and then glows bright for a moment. In those few dazzling seconds, she sees that the boxes containing her Christmases have gone. She slumps, face in hands, and remembers as she has been forced to remember every December these twelve years past. Though her eyes are closed, the pictures are clear. She is looking through the hatch into the house below, ceilings and walls and doors no barrier to her vision. She sees Jim being led from the house by their eldest daughter, his face haunted by confusion, not knowing what memories he has lost but feeling their absence all the same.

Where are you taking me?

We've explained it to you dad, remember – you can't look after yourself anymore.

Your mother, she…

The three daughters exchange glances. *Mum's gone dad.*

Gone. She is gone. She takes her hands from her face and looks at them. How can she be gone when she is still here – when she has been here all along? *I'm not gone*, she whispers.

The light begins to dim. She looks up at it and says, *not yet – please, just a few moments longer*, but the slow fade continues and the shadows creep forward. No-one is coming home for Christmas, not anymore. Just as the last of the light fades, she once again feels something flutter at her cheek and repeats the words, *there is nothing up here…*

The Upper Room

by Rieve Atkinson

I've been a dealer in second-hand and antiquarian books for some years now, but it wasn't a career I deliberately chose. The bookshop and its stock were left to me by the previous owner, who gave me regular part-time work there during the three years that I was studying at art college. We soon became friends, as well as colleagues, and she took the trouble to teach me a lot about her trade. When she became too ill to continue running the shop, I often visited her at her home and I like to think that she found comfort in the knowledge that I was looking after the premises in her absence, although I had no idea of her bequest to me. I could have sold the business immediately at a good price and set myself up with a decent studio, but despite my inexperience in money matters, I was sure that the bookshop would provide me with a more reliable income than my paintings might.

Time passed and I've done well here, thanks to the established clientele of my generous friend and to the central location of the premises, in the shadow of the castle walls, attracting tourists as well as collectors. I have learnt even more about old books and slowly built a reputation for paying a fair price, which means that I now do all my buying privately, not at auctions, and I've expanded the stock with a variety of prints and engravings, which are displayed on the ground floor. I've become a serious collector of books too, especially fine bindings, and this hobby of mine makes going out on book calls even more interesting. I keep my own collection on the top floor of the shop, together with any newly acquired stock awaiting research and pricing. It's only a small room approached by a steep, narrow staircase, so isn't suitable for a retail space, but it's high-ceilinged and fully shelved on three sides. The window under the eaves on the outer wall doesn't let in much light, although that's a good thing for book storage.

Just before Christmas, on two consecutive afternoons, a slender, elegant, elderly lady wearing a long, lilac coat of an old-fashioned style, her hair pinned up in a pleat, spent some time looking through the print troughs examining their contents slowly and carefully. On the second occasion, after she'd been in the shop for almost fifteen minutes, I asked her if there was anything in particular she was searching for. She didn't seem to mind my question and said that she had some prints she wanted to sell, but wasn't sure what type they were, or whether I'd want to buy them. I told her I'd certainly like to have a look, offering to call at her home to view them, but she didn't seem keen on that, saying she'd bring something in on the following day.

She arrived as promised, carrying a flat, oblong parcel wrapped in brown paper, telling me she'd decided to bring two prints because they were a pair. They turned out to be beautiful, but unsigned, gouache paintings of Lake Como. I explained about the medium used and she seemed very surprised. Apparently they had been in her family for a long time and were always referred to, by her parents, as prints. I offered her exactly half the amount I thought I could sell them for and got the immediate impression that it was far more than she'd expected to receive; at least, she accepted very quickly.

Over the next month, Miss Passat - which I discovered was her name - brought in two more gouaches, this time of the Italian Alps, and some hand-coloured antique maps showing different regions of France. I was happy to buy them all. After that, she said she'd no more pictures to sell, but did have three special books for me to look at, which she would bring soon. Bearing in mind the quality of her previous offerings, I was curious to see what they might be. This time she took longer to return but, in about a fortnight, she called again carrying a leather Gladstone bag, putting it on the edge of the central table before removing her gloves to open it and produce a carefully wrapped, largish book. Taking it from her, I paused thinking that there were more to come, but I was wrong. She obviously intended, as she had done with most of the pictures, to bring them in one at a time. This first one was a late Victorian edition of Brehm's 'Wild Life and Scenes in Many Lands', bound in a rather bizarre combination of dark green morocco with inlaid panels of horizontally mounted porcupine quills, on both boards. The second, when it came, dated from 1867 and was 'A Treatise on Herne's Oak' by William Perry, wood carver to Queen Victoria.

It had a label inside, pasted onto the front endpaper, certifying that the intricately decorated boards were carved from portions of wood from that famous tree. I paid Miss Passat very generously for both these unusual items, because I wanted them for my own collection.

Two days later she arrived with her third book, which really took my breath away; something I'd never expected to see, let alone handle. It was a copy of John Gay's 'Fables' probably dating from the early 1800s. Not a first edition, not scarce, and roughly demy octavo size, perhaps six by eight inches, but with charming wood-engraved illustrations by Thomas Bewick. It was bound in what I thought might be vellum, of a sort of honey or treacle colour, which had a certain luminosity about it. To my great surprise, a hand-written paper label, glued inside the front board, told me that it was 'Bound in the skin of John… executed for cowardice in the face of the enemy at the Battle of Toulouse'. There was no binder's ticket or bookseller's label and the man's surname had been neatly cut out. It had no other inscriptions. I'd read about examples of anthropodermic book bindings and their extreme rarity, so I told Miss Passat straight away that I couldn't possibly afford to buy this book, which was the sort of thing that should be in a museum. She said it was never her intention to sell it because her father had told her to do so would bring bad luck. She wanted to give it to me, if I would accept. Despite my almost overwhelming desire to possess it I tried hard to refuse, but she seemed determined to have her own way. With a pleading look in her watery, blue eyes, she said how disappointed she'd be if she couldn't find it an appreciative home and, eventually, I gave in. Apparently she knew nothing of its provenance, other than her father's ownership of it, but she suspected that it might originally have belonged to her grandfather, who was born in France but served as an officer in the British army.

After she'd gone, I sat at my desk with this wonderful item in front of me, finding it difficult to believe that it was now mine. The binding was striking in its simplicity and had four raised bands and a green lettering-piece on the spine, but no other decoration, it was extremely tactile in its smoothness. I knew that I was looking at the best find I'd ever have; the gem of my collection, far outshining anything other collectors might possess. Later, after locking up, I took my treasure to the upper room. I was tempted to take it home, but felt sure that its high value wouldn't be covered by my household insurance, yet I found it very difficult to leave behind and was awash with unfamiliar feelings of possessiveness and concern, in equal measure.

For the next few weeks, before I opened the shop and after I closed it, I went up to my book room just to look at, and touch, the Gay's 'Fables'. The compulsion to do this grew stronger and more frequent and began to be accompanied by my growing suspicion that, not only was I now no longer able to control this habit but also, whenever I held the book, that I was somehow being observed. I realise this sounds mildly neurotic, but it's true, and when in the top room I often looked behind me because the feeling of being watched was so strong. One morning I was convinced that someone, or something, was in the cupboard in the far corner, even though I knew it was crammed full of cardboard boxes and stationery supplies that I'd put there myself, and when I crept across the room and flung open the door, of course, nothing but paper and packaging spilled out onto the floor. I don't know that I ever really associated all these strange feelings directly with the 'Fables', more, I think, with my own imagination, but I did decide that I could probably do with a break from work, after the worst of the dark winter months. So, for the first five days of March, I closed the business and went to stay at a favourite hotel in Shanklin. Crossing on the Solent ferry made it seem that the distance travelled from my home was much further than it actually was, and although the weather wasn't good during my short holiday, it didn't really matter. My accommodation was luxurious, the meals outstanding, and I was able to spend a lot of time by a roaring fire in the resident's lounge reading, or else taking long country walks when the rain held off; hardly ever thinking of the most recent addition to my book collection.

I returned on a Sunday afternoon, having already decided that I'd go straight to the bookshop and deal with any post, rather than spending time on it when I re-opened the following day. The town was quiet and in the grip of a clinging sea-mist creeping through its narrow streets. There were only a few book enquiries and a couple of bills on the mat inside the shop door. First I checked to see if the books that had been requested were in stock or needed to be added to my search list. Then, armed with a mug of coffee, sat at my desk to write cheques but I soon noticed a repetitive sound which seemed to be coming from the first floor. Looking up the staircase I couldn't see anything amiss, but the sound most resembled drips muffled by falling on carpet, or cloth of some sort, so I climbed the stairs to the landing where, on the left, is a small cloakroom containing a hand basin and lavatory; the only upstairs room that has any plumbing. I looked around in there very carefully, but found nothing that might be causing the noise which I could still hear and, if anything, seemed slightly louder than before. I crossed the landing into the larger room opposite, where less expensive stock is displayed, and there on the carpet in the middle of the floor beneath the light fitting, was a large, dark patch of wetness. I knelt down to look at it closely and although I could have seen more clearly if I'd switched the light on, obviously it wasn't safe to do so, but I could see, and smell, enough to know that this wasn't just water. Then, as I stood up, I completely lost my grip on reality.

I was suddenly pushed from behind, by an immensely strong and irresistible force, towards the stairs leading to the upper room. A cold, hard column extending down the whole length of my spine, held me rigid and powerless. I felt completely paralysed and transformed into prey, as if from the poisonous bite of a spider.

Nevertheless, I was slowly propelled across the floor, then up the staircase. Terror flooded through me; my teeth were chattering uncontrollably and my eyelids fluttering, but I couldn't close my eyes or turn my head. The propulsive power of the icy pillar at my back drove my body upwards and, as I reached the very top, it began to turn me, forcing me to face into the room. There in the centre of that room, was a truly horrific sight. Suspended by a noose of coarse rope, tied onto an iron hook embedded in the ceiling, was the cadaver of a man. He was dressed only in old-fashioned, military-style, grey trousers and shiny, black, ankle boots. His naked back faced me; he had been brutally flayed. An oblong section of skin, between the bottom of his shoulder blades and his waist had been removed, exposing bright, raw flesh, constantly oozing blood which gathered into droplets, ran down his trousers, and dripped onto the floor.

As the size and shape of that wound burned into my mind, the nausea and hyperventilation of sudden shock almost overwhelmed me. In this extremity of fear I experienced everything in front of me in sharp detail; smelt the man's ripe, yeasty sweat, saw the dry, scaly skin of his elbows, the glistening lymph on the exposed dermis, the purple bruising on his neck just below the noose, the pale light illuminating his left side, the way that the toes of his boots turned inwards, almost touching together. Then, and I could hardly believe my eyes, I saw his right leg move slightly and realised that he was still alive; had been flayed alive! I heard an unmistakable creak from the rope as his body started to revolve very slowly, bringing his right ear into view and I knew, at any moment, I would see his face.

That's the last thing I remember before regaining consciousness at the bottom of the stairs. My head ached and I had such a piercingly sharp pain in my left shoulder that I couldn't move my arm at all, but I didn't care much about that; my main aim was to escape from the shop as quickly as possible. I stumbled downstairs and out onto the street, making for the pub on the corner, hammering on the side door, praying that someone would hear me. The landlord's wife took me straight to the local hospital, while her husband went back to make the bookshop secure. I didn't attempt to tell anyone what had really taken place; just that I'd tripped and fallen down the stairs.

When I went back to the shop some days later, my brother, a level-headed engineer, drove me there. Tom, who'd heard the full story, although I'm not sure how much of it he actually believed, led the way to the upper room. There were no bloodstains, no ropes or hooks; nothing to indicate that anything untoward, supernatural or otherwise, had happened, but being in that space again made me feel threatened and afraid, and I could still detect the metallic odour of blood, even though my brother said he couldn't smell anything except musty old books. I couldn't bring myself to touch the Gay's 'Fables', so I handed Tom a glove to wear whilst he removed it from the shelf, and gave him a bag to carry it in. Without a thought about its scarcity or value, I told him to burn it as soon as possible. He promised he would: I hope he's kept his word.

My dislocated shoulder soon improved, and I've gone back to work. I'd like to say that things have returned to normal, but that's not true. I don't use the upper room anymore, it's permanently locked, and I no longer collect fine bindings, my interest now is in illustrated books, which I keep at home. I've also altered my opening hours so that, even in winter, I'm not in the shop after dark, and when I get back to my house I leave lights on in all the rooms, especially when I go to bed, because the thought of waking in darkness terrifies me. That feeling of being watched still happens, and not just in the bookshop. When I'm alone, anywhere, it can crawl into my consciousness and start to control me, but I'm receiving regular therapy to help me cope with this.

Although this is a small town, and I couldn't possibly mistake her neat figure in its old-fashioned clothes, I've never seen Miss Passat again, and I don't know what I would say to her if I did. I often wonder why she was so eager for me to accept the 'Fables' and whether the execution of that man could possibly have been ordered by her grandfather, but she'd told me she had lived with that book all her life and surely couldn't have done so if she'd ever seen that awful, gory apparition that I was forced to witness; the memory of which, I know, will never leave me.

The Great Unknown
by Craig Aitchison
(3ʳᵈ Place)

When light fell upon him and Sir Walter Scott awoke, mind clear of laudanum and shocked awake by pain, he knew for certain that he was dying. There was no treatment, no tincture or treatment that would help - no last minute reprieve, no heroic rescue. It was merely a matter of time.

He lay in bed and listened. At first the room seemed silent, then through the open window the breeze carried the liquid hush of the Tweed. Scott hauled his body into a sitting position and looked through the window, past the garden wall. On the river, a heron turned its head and, as if aware of being watched, took to flight, stuttering at first then gliding through the air, leading Scott's gaze to the trees and the hills beyond.

How he longed to walk out there, with dear old Tom has he had done so often. As they walked, Tom would recite snatches of ballads or talked about the estate, his wife and bairns, in that plain, honest way that Scott never found amongst men of letters or law - the way he had spoken to Scott in the Sherriff Court while being tried for poaching fish - *There's plenty mair there, sir. I hae mouths tae feed.* There was no shame in his eyes, just defiance, a bare-faced act of insubordination. Scott offered him a job that day; they had been friends ever since. But now Tom was gone. They would walk together no more.

Lacking the strength to stay upright, he settled back into his cushions, looking at the ceiling bosses - fleur-de-lis, rose, lion and above his own place at the table, a cabbage. A joke at his own expense; he was a simple man. The decorations were made of wood, painted to look like stone engravings, a facsimile of the antique.

At first his request to have the bed brought here, with the view of the river, was met with looks of puzzlement but after the doctor had whispered in the ear of Anne, his daughter, it was done. While the dining table was removed, Scott spent some time in the library, thumbing histories, romances and collections of poetry, volumes in French, Latin and German. There were books that he had loved, books that had brought a tear to his eye and books which he'd read to his children. Many had faded from his memory; many would never be read.

His finger fell upon a slim volume, Trinum Magicum. He thrilled at simply holding it, knowing the danger it held, the forbidden enchantment. He did not open the book - its magic could rest between the worn covers.

There was a clatter from the study next door, a curse, 'Christ, man,' that was immediately hushed by another. The corridors were narrow, the bed large and heavy. Scott smiled, amused rather than offended, pleased that he could still cause a little fuss even now.

The bed had been moved and here he had lain for some days now, occasionally being fed by Anne, who cradled his head and tipped the spoon to his mouth. The draught tasted of bitter ashes.

Yet, this was the room where he had dined like a king on dishes of vegetables grown on the grounds, princely venison shot in the moors, noble salmon fished from the river, washed down with wine, sherry and port. Guests gathered to swap tales and to toast Scott's success. So many toasts; so much success. The learned and powerful had travelled from all over the country, and beyond, to eat, drink and talk. Their names flitted before Scott, then disappeared like dust motes in the air. The artist whose face shone when he talked about light, darkened when the conversation turned to money. The poet who kept calling Scott 'The

Wizard', come to steal his magic. The stammerer who sang with a voice like silk. An English poet who had been gentle in his manners until he had savoured a little too much hospitality and lifted a claymore from the armoury and overbalanced, sprawling on the floor, giggling. The shepherd who brought songs and the tangy scent of hard work. So much to feed upon, to savour.

> *In Hermitage they sat at dine*
> *In pomp and proud array*
> *And oft they fill'd the blood-red wine*
> *While merry minstrels play.*
> *Then turned to plaintive strains their tongue*
> *'Of Scotland's love and lee'*

Scott had been at the centre of it all, but even then, when he was sought out and lauded, he felt distant, listening and observing those around him like one of the grotesques in the ceiling, all eyes and ears. He had craved solitude – peace from empty flattery, or the particulars of the law. Now he was alone and filled with empty dread.

> *As I walk by myself*
> *I talked to myself*
> *And thus myself said to me.*

This house had been his refuge, his conundrum castle, where Scott had escaped the bustle and grime of Edinburgh for this home by the river, often delighting more in the company of dogs than men. Dear Maida, that most faithful and worthy companion, who'd stayed by his side on the moor and in the study. He had found peace here, and the fountain of inspiration flowed, pouring forth line after line and book after book. Wealth followed, and fame. The more the clamour grew, the more he craved the silence to write.

With success, Scott's wealth grew and so he poured it into his greatest creation - this house, once only a humble farmhouse, but now a wondrous conundrum castle. He built crenulations and battlements, stained glass windows and a chapel. He surrounded it with statues, a garden in the Italian style and another which provided fruit and vegetables and a forest of trees and shrubs both native and exotic. His family grew too; this was their playground and their schoolhouse. Scott filled the house with souvenirs from all over the country and beyond, things owned or carried by Wallace, Rob Roy, Bonnie Prince Charlie. How he wished these objects could tell their stories. A wisp of hair from the head of Mary Queen of Scots, kept in a locket. An assemblage of curiosities unlike any other.

Tom asked Scott once how he knew they were genuine.

I have it on good authority.

Aye, but how dae ye ken?

He did not know. Not for certain.

For a moment, Scott felt the urge to push himself up and to hold one of those precious objects, feeling its authenticity: the fine broadsword, the flintlock from the Battle of Waterloo, the lock of Flora McDonald's hair. But these gewgaws would not give him as much solace as the memory of ruffling the curls of his grandson, little Johnnie. Dear, sweet boy.

Scott tried to summon the wonderful, spontaneous jingle of the boy's laughter. But it would not come. Like so many things, the sound was lost forever. Johnnie had been gone nine months now and Scott's response had been to pour more words forth, though the fountain had surely now run dry; each scrawl now dragged from deep within. Scott had vowed to repay his debts with his own right hand, but how weak the fingers that held his pen - each leaf scratched with pain as surely as if he wrote in blood. Had he ever been The Wizard who conjured tales with his quill? Had he stood at the side of an English King dressed in tartan while pipes skirled about them? Had he walked the hills, seeking out ballads, bracing himself against a gale, clutching a discovery in his pocket? For now, Scott was a pale, thin, shambling revenant.

As a boy, just a few minutes over Edinburgh cobbles had made him hobble painfully, but here he could walk for miles, clutching the hand of his grandfather who sang in his hushed, deep tones. In these Border braes and in their stories, Scott found the place he would make his home.

Years later, in these troubled times, he needed the comfort of the gardens, the trees and the hills. Charlotte was gone. His money too. And though he was still the laird here in Abbotsford, the outside world was in turmoil.

Scott recalled the day he travelled to Jedburgh to cast his vote in the Election. The girls had tried to persuade him not to go: he was not fit for the journey and there was much talk of unrest, but he must do his duty. For the most part, things had passed off peacefully. No doubt the dragoons stationed on Ancrum bridge did much to convince the gathering, although large, to content itself with much clamour and no great mischief.

It was a long difficult day, but Scott prepared to depart content that the vote had gone the right way, the passing of Reform delayed, the behemoth of Progress held at bay a little longer. As he approached his carriage however, a faction shouted abuse at him. For the most part, they were at a distance, but one pushed his way forward, standing between Scott and his carriage.

'You're done, Sir' the man slurred. Spittle shot from his mouth – the unwashed, uneducated face of fury, of the future. The man mimed rope going around his neck, pulling tight, eyes bulging. Scott tried to find a word, something to say, some connection to make with this man but he could not so he brushed past, steadied himself with his stick and clambered aboard the carriage, relieved to be bound for home. The ride home pained him, jarring his bad leg and unsettling his stomach.

> *This night is my departing night.*
> *For here nae langer must I stay;*
> *There's neither friend nor foe o'mine,*
> *But wishes me away.*

Scott had rocked with rage until Anne came to him. There's no wisdom in a mob, she said and stroked his brow. Gentle, wise Anne. He longed to ring the bell, to summon her to play the harp for him but could not remember if she was still here or was gone. It was so difficult to hold on.

His body convulsed with pain and he screwed shut his eyes, forcing a single word from his lips. *Help.*

His vision blurred so that he could no longer see the river beyond the window, nor even the window itself, or the room he lay in and his eyes and mind were filled with a terrible blackness. There was a falling away, like he was on board a ship dropping from the crest of a great wave, into a dark, bottomless trough.

Falling.

He felt a strong hand take his. Tom.

Scott was certain that that this hand was Tom's. His dear friend was here now, a smile on his face, like sunlight on a rugged moor. *Come away sir.*

Couldn't Tom see that he was ill? Scott lifted his hand to wave away the stick that Tom held towards him but when he did, he realised that he felt no stiffness, no nausea, no pain. What Scott could feel was the coarse, slick tongue of a dog on his hand.

Maida. She nuzzled him, pushing him upright with ease. His legs felt strong, ready to follow Tom across the floor, to explore, to stride out surrounded by the scamper and fervour of dogs – not just Maida, but Spice, Camp, Nimrod and Ginger too – that carried him to the door and the paths and the rolling hills beyond, to the scent of ripening fruit and the late blossom of the forest flowers, to the brush of heather on shins and to the bright autumn sun that glistened on the slow-flowing waters.

The Abbey

by Eoin Gough

Usually old Bassett, a man of broad chest and broader appetite, would bellow "Have ye no homes to go to?" come closing time and would hurry patrons out the door as his broad smile pulled up his rosy jowls. Then Liam and the others would sit at the bar and have a nightcap before setting off. In other bars in the village, those frequented by fishermen and sailors, The Bowline and The Catspaw, drinks could be had by staff and a few locals deep into the early morning, but old Bassett was unyielding in his rule: in The Abbey it was one drink and out before midnight. The license ran to half past eleven, and he locked the door himself with a great brass key that looked as though it belonged to a different century.

Bassett had a funny fastidiousness about him. He would pace the room carefully before closing up and move furniture until it was just so as if a spark from the greying embers in the fire might leap out over the stone floor and catch a bare wooden table leg and turn the place into an inferno. Sometimes he would lock and unlock the door several times until he felt sure the bolt had driven home. After that he would cross himself and say goodnight, no one ever said outright that you mustn't leave before this ritual was completed, but it wouldn't have felt right.

On a night like Christmas Eve though, Liam imagined old Bassett would keep it gentle.

There were sure to be only a few of the old fellows who would need the nudge and a gentle word to get them out the door. There are those at Christmas who have no one waiting at home and he was always mindful, old Bassett: he knew his work. Despite his powerful build, he had near never been called upon to use force in his long tenure.

It was still afternoon and the smell of cloves wended its way from the ancient vault of the stone kitchen and mingled with rich turfy smoke off the fires and the bright happy laughter of anticipation. The windows in the front let in the last pure white winter light. Soon, it would melt into the comfortable incandescence of soft electric light and scattered candles. Liam was pouring pints and watching as Marianne busied herself lighting the candles. The comings and goings of half the village passed through The Abbey on this last day before Christmas and, with the arrival of road-sore but smiling travellers, many blithe spirited reunions went on round the oaken tables laden with ales, ciders, stouts and shorts.

Bassett turned towards Liam. "Travellers returning from faraway places, bringing the good with smiles on their faces."

"What's that from?"

"It's from old Bassett." the heavyset man said with a chuckle that shook his full weight.

Liam gave him the beginnings of a perplexed look and was about to inquire further when a customer came over, looking for menus.

Down below in the kitchen, hams were baking, criss-crossed with cloves pricking into the fat, steaming brussels sprouts were bathing in knobs of melting butter and endless potatoes were roasting all day. Chef carved plate after plate of turkey, and the shelves of the cold room had several trifles. Christmas puddings that had been laid down the year before were being opened and fried in whisky before being brought up above with fresh whipped cream.

"It's a wonder," Liam had observed earlier, "that people can't wait for the real day."

Bassett had smiled at him and said, "there's plenty for who this is the real day. Not everyone has a mammy like yours, young master Liam."

True enough, he'd thought, and then wondered if Bassett had a family to go to but didn't ask. They were overrun, the place was packed not so much as it might be on a New Year's Eve at midnight, but in a sustained way where every table was taken and little groups stood chatting, drinks in their hands. It began at noon and continued right through without slowing. He poured out hot whiskeys, Irish coffees and mulled wine from a great tureen to warm up weary shoppers back in from the city. Old fellows were drinking pint after pint of stout and the young people were on lagers, wines and ales. A busy day behind the bar it might have been, but busier still for the serving staff who were running up and down between the lounge and the kitchen all day. Liam watched the plates passing and ached for the moment tomorrow when he could cut into his own Christmas dinner.

It struck him, as he went back and forth from the till to the bar where crowds of faces awaited his attention, that the bar was such an utterly different place after closing. All the little cubbies with tucked away tables and snugs in which people laughed so merrily would empty and the people trying to catch his eye would depart, but somehow the feeling of their presence never walked out the door with them. They left behind the echo of someone watching you, the echo of someone waiting. But of course there was no one there. Maybe that was why old Bassett never settled for looking over the place just once but had to do the circuit again and again until he was at last satisfied. Even the light would change and when Liam looked at his own face in the mirror above the till, he couldn't take it in whole. It felt like his eyes were drawn to the lines and creases in his skin, to the pores and blemishes. Enough to make the figure in the mirror a stranger.

"Is Santie bringing you anything nice Liam?" This was Marianne, she was close to his age and had dark hair and sea-blue eyes.

He looked up from washing glasses and said, "I just wrote in my letter I'd like some new socks and a surprise."

"Well, I hope Liam that you are most pleasantly surprised," she said, lingering and wiping the bar with a cloth.

"What about you, expecting anything special?"

Marianne sighed gravely, saying with faux levity, "my wishes almost never come true. What can Santa do for so tragic a figure as I?" before pretending to swoon and letting forth an unrestrained laugh.

"Oh, really? Weren't you good this year?" Liam asked.

Her eyebrows shot up and Marianne slapped him lightly on the arm. "I will have you know. I am always on my very best behaviour. The nerve of some people."

Marianne walked away with a haughty overproud step descending towards the kitchen without looking back. As Liam returned to serving, he remembered the weekend he was put working in the kitchen. It was oppressive. The whole thing was underground, and the walls were bare stone. It had a vaulted ceiling and was reputed to be part of the original abbey, built hundreds of years before. No one else seemed to feel the way the stones gripped you on every side almost ready to suffocate you. In the cold room, where usually they kept meat hanging on great hooks, Liam recalled feeling sick at the sight of it. Meat was a normal part of his diet but, after seeing it hanging there still on the bone, the image kept coming back to him of a human body cut in half and hanging on a hook. For weeks every time he ate meat, it felt like he was chewing on flesh.

A spry older man with thick greying hair and a worn heavy winter coat came in with a package wrapped in brown paper and finished with a bow under his arm. Liam recognised him at once as Nolan; he wasn't sure what he did for a living, but he seemed to have a hand in many things. The fishermen all knew him and he was respected in the rougher dockside bars. His family was more than a family: it was an extended clan, and through them he was known to the whole of the wider area. The village was situated on the northern side of a broad peninsula. The Abbey was in the centre of the village above the harbour, but during a storm you could still hear the blast of the roiling black waters of the Irish sea. Nolan was popular even among the old biddies, who loved him because he could read their palms as though they were still young and full of dance.

Nolan was one who dealt in fortunes and favour, past and future. If you asked him, he'd have said he could tell you no more than you knew yourself about the future. But there was something uncanny in what he could uncover, he would know before an expectant mother if she were to have a boy or a girl, and he could tell a stranger where they had been born and their mother's name. As to the past, he knew every tall-tale, anecdote, history and myth of the hill of Howth and much else besides. Sitting down by the fire with a friend, he might begin a story and by the end have half the pub gathered round to hear it finished. Although he was not an entertainer, old Bassett always gave him the first drink on the house as though he were there to play music, and after that Liam had never seen him need to look to his own pocket for a drink.

That's not to say he was mean; Nolan very often left Liam and the others a generous tip and would always see those in want were got a glass of something by the fire.

Liam made to bring a pint over to Nolan; he always had a Smithwicks, and there was no need for him to come to the bar to order. But he was intercepted by a squat woman of about forty with bird's nest hair and a colourful scarf breaking the drabness of her coat.

"What time is he expected? Are we still safe?" her eyes were too far open and blinked insistently.

"I'm sorry, who?" As Liam asked this, Marianne swept the Smithwicks from the bar and brought it over to Nolan as a broad expectant grin cracked over his lips. Marianne's dark hair fell from behind her ear as she bent low to hear some whispered kindness, and then she let out a squeal and a laugh. Liam's eye left her and returned to the woman. "I'm sorry, what?"

Her doe eyes were hazel, and she spoke reproachfully. "You know who I am talking about. Is it safe? Has he come? I'll have to go if he's to come soon."

"Do you mean Nolan?" asked Liam, looking back towards the fire where he sat with a friend.

"I mean him as has no name to utter."

Old Bassett stepped forward and greeted the woman who he recognised. "Don't mind her Liam, she's an old stoat winding you up. Now, what can I get you, Nell?"

The woman looked agitated and held her gaze on Liam a moment but then accepted a gin and tonic before stalking away to talk to another woman. It was clear from the way the other looked back they were speaking badly about him. These things can happen when there is drink had.

Having been slightly unnerved he took his break. Though he didn't smoke, Liam always kept a lighter in his pocket for the patrons, and he walked out the front door to breathe the sea air for a few moments. A number of the customers were out having cigarettes around a few wooden barrels left outside for this purpose. Leaning against the wall, he watched a while as a light dusting of snow drifted over the village and did its best to stick. But, under the strings of electric lights, the carollers and locals walking past, meeting serendipitously, and embracing brought too heavy a footfall for the snow to catch. There was time enough to hear a few bars of a few songs as the carollers crooned door-to-door, collecting money for some good cause.

Below, the harbour lay still, and the shops had now closed. The little tracts of snow built up in patches of grass, gutters and on windowsills made the light seem cleaner and Liam let out a breath that came on like a cloud of smoke. At the doorway, he remembered the night that he and Bassett had been a few minutes late closing up and Bassett had been so rattled that he clean fell off the step and needed Liam to haul him back to his feet. For a moment he'd lain there as still as the grave and Liam had been worried, before he said "don't touch me, don't touch me. Give me a moment. Just a moment is all."

Walking back into the warmth was a delight right down to the bones. Customers were everywhere and old Bassett shouted over to him to go out and get a keg. There was not a hint of reproach in his voice. He was never fazed by a heavy trade, just worked a little faster and saw to everyone quick as he could.

Bar work in Liam's opinion was a grand line of work; he liked every bit of it, even the changing of the kegs. The Abbey had three log fires on the ground floor: one in the front bar and two in the lounge. Patrons coming in out of the cold could be seen to visibly grow taller and expand in the face of the heat, weary shoulders and hearts were warmed and renewed in minutes; the only drawback to this was when it got busy and you were on your feet, it could get uncomfortably warm. That's why he took his break outside and now the chance to run out the back for another minute and cool down: well it was money in the bank. He walked out the back door with the old keg, passed through the yard and came to the cellar door where he could collect a new keg and for a moment, his thoughts. The cool night air traced goosepimples on his narrow bare forearms. Where the work of a thousand nights had made old Bassett's forearms look like rope twisted around the bough of a tree, at twenty Liam's own arms were still adjusting to manhood. That's not to say he couldn't manage the heavy work handily. In the dark and shadowed cellar, thick with cobwebs, he made to take up a keg when outside he heard a rustle. Taking two steps back up the stair he spied an old fellow in a woollen jacket and a collarless shirt out to answer the call of nature.

"The gents is inside." he called out and the man looked over to him and his eyes flitted up past his shoulder. A look of mute feral fear seized him and with the light from one side and the dark from the other the old man's own eyes seemed hollow and black like a skull. He raised his finger as though something in the cellar behind Liam was pulling and stretching his very bones.

Liam turned and, seeing nothing but darkness, said, "ah yeah, pull the other one," uncertainly. But behind him he heard the old man running and a toothless cry that sounded as dull as the fall of a hammer on earth. As Liam regained himself the man was gone but he felt his own breath was ragged. He quickly pulled a fresh keg and heaved it up the stairs and closed the door with a shudder.

Inside, he passed by Nolan's table where a large group had congregated. Nolan was telling dark stories of ships and the sea: men hanged by the yardarm and men whose very lives hung by a prayer out on the rolling seas. Stories of the women who waited ashore for them and the children who died never knowing their fathers. Of triumphs and defeats he told them. Stories like paths well-walked, he brought out, fresh and new and, though he had walked them many times, his face was still burdened by the loss and his voice still chastened.

Moving past, Liam caught a little of a story about a developer well known in those parts "though I'll not share his name" who, when digging up a foundation for his mansion, found the bones of a full battle. Whether it was Vikings or the pirate queen Grace O'Malley he couldn't say, but "there was blood in the very stones".

Liam pushed on with the keg trying to make a path through the patrons. He brushed past the Christmas tree which had tinsel and little glass ornaments old Bassett brought down from the attic once a year and to top it off a most beautiful angel that Liam's grandmother held kept out dark spirits. At the tables around the tree, Liam saw people young and old in conversation. The whole of the village was mixing in a great festive churn: a twenty-year-old might be listening in rapt attention to a sixty-year-old who had come up and asked, "are you a Kelly? Aye? I know your father. Sit a while, I'll buy you a drink."

There was a bone-deep satisfaction in the way all were together joined in kindness, understanding and good cheer. Liam shook off the memory of the old man who had startled him outside and disappeared back into the crowd. It was coming in on last orders and, though Liam couldn't hear, a young girl of about fifteen was talking to Nolan, having got him alone.

"And can you see the future?"

"Only so much as the future will let me see."

"But how does it even work?"

"It's more a feeling, a sense, than a true sight."

"Could you talk to the dead?"

"I wish I could tell you yes, for I know why you're asking, but I'll tell you I'm glad I can't. And I know that your father will be looking down on you tonight. As he does every single night," he added darkly, for Nolan's stories always were tinted with darkness. "Truly, I'm glad I can't. There are people I've met, the ones who brought me up to tell tales, well, they could tell you things known only in hell."

Just then as he spoke the word, across the room, the glass Liam took from the shelf exploded and shards went crashing to the ground. A ragged cheer went up and a few claps, but the heart of the pub was in good spirits and did not make the most of the poor boy as he swept up the broken glass. There was that and the fact old Bassett heard the noise of it and when he looked up the knife slipped in his hand while he was cutting lemons and he cut into his index finger deeply. Bassett wrapped a cloth round it and continued working without a word.

Customers started leaving and Marianne, Liam, Bassett and the rest of the staff began clearing up. You could see some of them stumbling, half-cut, every intention of going to the midnight mass.

"What happened to your hand?" asked Marianne.

"It'll keep." said Bassett with a slight grimace.

Liam came over to him. "Show us a look, boss."

Bassett reluctantly pulled back the cloth. The knife had cut very deep down into the knuckle.

There was a lot of blood, and the tip of his finger was hanging by a thread.

Liam shook his head. "You're going to have to go to the doctor. I can lock up."

"I'll see he gets everything cleared up," added Marianne, cheerfully because she hadn't seen the cut.

Seamus, another barman, took Bassett in the car, and the great brass key was left by the till for Liam. Soon the last patrons were on their way out the door.

Nolan, who knew Liam through his uncle, stopped by the bar and looked at Liam before saying carefully, "don't tarry, young Conroy. It wouldn't do to stay past midnight." He gave a knock on the wooden bar for good luck and dropped a few coins.

"I have no intention of staying," said Liam with a smile. "Thanks. And merry Christmas."

With that, Nolan went out and began his walk home up the hill. Marianne and Liam were left alone: the remaining staff being in a rush home to their families. Liam poured them each a whiskey because it was late, and because he'd promised Bassett to leave by midnight. They downed them and Liam left the glasses turned upside down on a drip tray to be dealt with later. They put on their coats and made for the door. In the hesitation of a boy and a girl looking into each other's eyes, the moment seemed to unfold for something to happen. They moved towards each other. But there was a crash from within and the spell was broken.

"It's probably something off the tree. I'd better check: it was near the fire. You can wait outside. I'll walk you home."

Marianne said, "all right. Don't be long." She walked out the door to the soft falling snow which deadened the sounds of the street.

Inside, Liam trotted over to the Christmas tree and heard outside as the church bells began to toll the midnight mass. The angel had fallen from its perch and shattered. With the bells still tolling, he checked the cubbies and the snug for anyone forgotten inside. Finding no one but feeling in the back of his neck he was being watched, he grabbed the dustpan and brush and returned. When he was up close, he got this strange smell: a cloying, sweet smell, that caught in his craw. As the last bell sounded, Liam got a crawling feeling on his skin. He really shouldn't be here: he'd promised. The door, and Marianne beyond it, was only a few feet away but, even before he took a step towards it, he knew something would pull him back.

There was a sound coming from out in the yard. It was half-hummed and sweet like an almost forgotten lullaby or a word stuck on the tip of your tongue. It could have been singing or even laughing. Whatever it was was just below his hearing. He turned on the lights of the back corridor and walked out into the yard. It was empty. He took a few paces, almost retracing the old man's steps when he'd come out looking for the toilets. Then, he turned. The cellar door was open, and he saw it: what the old man had seen.

Marianne waited outside through the sounding of the bell and heard the soft slow sea down the hill. She waited and saw a rook alight on the string of Christmas lights. Marianne waited, and waited, and waited. Then, finally, there was a noise from inside beyond the unlocked door.

A Better Place

by Estrella Burgess

(Children's Runner-Up)

The air was piercing, setting an icy chill upon the town.

Shop windows blaze alight in hopes of last-minute Christmas shoppers and houses adorned with snow, wore it as a Lady would her finest furs.

*

A mother, draping stockings above a crackling fire and children tucked away in their beds, trying their hardest to fall asleep.

Only something was missing.

It was only a few months before had she received the telegram, branded with the words "missing in action".

This news only created uncertainty and worry, yet upon receiving the letter she did what all mothers do best, act as though nothing has happened for the sake of her children.

So, she'd stowed it away in her sewing tin and continued as normal.

Eleanor Devitt leans back in her chair, emotionally exhausted.

It seemed especially hard to stay positive at this time of year, as it had always been a special season to her and her husband.

She lets her mind drift, delving deep into her memories.

Suddenly, she is awoken from her thoughts by the sound of the snow, the crisp, crunching sound it makes when a boot falls upon it.

She gets to her feet, walking to the window but before she makes it there, she hears a sharp rapping upon the old Beech door.

Before she answers it however, she calls out "Who is it?".

No answer.

At that she slowly and carefully unlatches the bolt and pulls the door open.

There, stood before her, is the face she thought she'd never see again.

"Edward!" she cries, rushing into his arms, "You're freezing" she exclaims and leads him to the hearth, gesturing for him to remove his boots.

Yet upon looking up she sees his smile falter and his hazel eyes hold no reflection of the warm fire before them.

He was fading; like the moon when the sun begins to rise, dematerializing before her eyes. She attempts to embrace him once more, yet in vain for it is too late.

Eleanor is left there, nothing but thin air between her arms, tears streaming down her face.

*

As she retires to her sleeping quarters, she has one thought that helps her get a good night's rest; She knows now where he is...

...A better place.

.

Seven-Thirty at the Abbey

by Sue Roberts

Ellie waited impatiently at the entrance to Bryndhale Abbey. It was nearly time and he wasn't usually late. Had the train been held up? It was a tradition to meet at 7:30pm, as it was dark then at this time of year and no one else would be up at the Abbey, so they had it to themselves. Was that the train whistle? He wouldn't be long now, only a few minutes' walk from the station, although in this weather it might take him longer.

She looked around her and then up towards the Abbey ruins. It was today; 800 years ago, that Lady Matilda Beaufitz was supposed to have met a grisly end at these very ruins. Of course, the Abbey wasn't in ruins then, it was run by an evil abbot, who preyed on young women who came to him for help. Ellie pictured him twirling his black moustache and then decided that wouldn't look right on a monk. He had tried to have his wicked way with Lady Matilda and killed her when she attempted to run away. Her ghost had wandered the ruins ever since on the anniversary of her death.

They had all loved this local legend when they were at school together. They used to meet up here and scare themselves silly, the same group every time. Over the years, many of them had moved away for university or jobs, Kai amongst them, although he'd only gone to live in the next town, in a flat above his shop. For the last three years though, it had just been her and Kai, everyone else must have 'grown-up' and become very serious. Ellie laughed to herself, she firmly believed that growing up didn't mean you had to stop having fun.

She caught sight of Kai, walking silently up the hill through the snow and smiled. She might have known he'd never let her down.

'Hi there. I thought you weren't going to make it for a while' she shouted. It sounded too loud for the quiet night; everything was muffled in the blankets of snow, including his reply.

'What did you say?' she almost whispered as he drew level with her.

'You know I'd never let you down,' he said gently.

She grinned at him and turned to lead him up, where the path would normally have been if it wasn't covered in snow, to the Abbey. The nearer they got to it, the more they could see that the moon was shining directly through the main arched window, no glass left of course. It was beaming a ray of moonlight straight down onto where the main altar would have been.

'That's weird' she said, 'You don't think wicked Abbot Hugo sacrificed her there do you?'

'Ellie…' said Kai, shaking his head slowly.

'It's okay, I think we've established that he strangled her and threw her in the dungeons' she laughed although, of course, it would have been no laughing matter for Lady Matilda. He had bricked her body up somewhere in the walls afterwards, according to the local stories told in the guidebook. She knew Kai didn't really believe all this stuff, but he always enjoyed the winter excursion to the ruins, it was fun. She thought he did it mostly for her sake though, she had to admit.

They walked on slowly and silently, while Ellie sneaked a glance at her companion. He seemed older since he'd started running that shop and he was working too hard. He looked grey against the whiteness of the snow but still handsome with the starry clear sky behind his head. Why had they never got together? Maybe it was because they'd always been good friends and it would ruin that? She was happy as they were anyway.

Reaching the chancel area, they stopped and admired the stars above them. It was so clear. Ellie felt like there ought to be a wind howling or thunder and lightning to make it more spooky, but she shivered just the same. Kai watched her and started to take his coat off before he stopped in his tracks and looked at her. She laughed at him. She always called him her gallant knight and knew that he would have faced the cold rather than let her shiver. She held her hand up.

'Don't. I'm not shivering with cold, it's just the atmosphere here.'

They trudged through the snow, round to the other side of the Abbey where the other ruined buildings were, and Ellie led the way to the corner. It was completely cut off from the moonlight in that corner. It didn't seem as if any light could penetrate it, the shadows were deeper than anywhere else. They went beyond dark.

Ellie moved towards it hesitantly and turned to say something to Kai. She found he hadn't moved an inch. He was just staring ahead.

'Kai,' she shouted, 'don't leave me to do this alone. I know I like being scared but I don't like doing this bit by myself. Thank you!'

He had started walking towards her, thank goodness. She needed to feel him there by her side, she didn't think she could do this if he stopped coming too – and it was just a bit of fun, a tradition they'd started. It was strange tonight though, stranger than normal and Kai had a face like a wet weekend. He'd hardly changed his expression since she'd first seen him tonight. She felt a tug of remorse at her insensitivity. Something might have happened at home or more likely he was working too hard. She wished that he'd slow down.

They both reached the corner together and edged slowly to the worn and ancient steps that had led down to the fateful dungeon. It was like being an impressionable child again, the feeling of someone being there, someone not of this world. She couldn't shake it and was glad she had Kai beside her. She could feel him at her shoulder.

Suddenly, it felt like the world was turning upside down. She flung her arms out but nothing was there to take hold of. Then she felt Kai's strong hands on her, pulling her back and into his arms. Not a bear hug like she felt she needed but a very gentle hug, while at the same time he pulled her right away from the dungeon steps and into the fresh night air again. She felt a kiss, like a whisper, just brush her cheek, then he stepped back, his eyes tightly closed and his head drooped towards his chest.

'Kai, you saved me from the same fate as Matilda!' she laughed, albeit shakily. She just felt relief and realised that maybe it wasn't the best idea to go near the steps on a night like tonight. Was it ice or mud she'd slipped on? It was almost as if something was drawing her down there. Pulling at her. Could Matilda have been responsible? She shook off the ridiculous notion. There was one thing, Kai wasn't grey anymore, he was as white as the snow and was just staring at her now. He was probably angry with her and she couldn't blame him.

'Kai, it's okay, I promise I won't go there anymore if it makes you feel any better. You look worse than I do!' She leaned into him and whispered, 'thanks for saving my life.'

Kai turned without a word and started walking away towards the Abbey gates. Ellie followed him, annoyed that she'd cut short the time they had together with her silliness. They didn't see each other much now and she vowed to herself that she would change that from now on.

As they walked towards the gate with silent footsteps, she looked up into the sky and saw strange-coloured clouds, heavy with snow. She would just get back in time. As she lowered her head again, she caught sight of something near the Abbey, something white, glowing, ethereal. The moonlight? No, it moved, hanging, gliding and then paused. Not a recognisable shape but a …presence was the nearest thing that came to Ellie's shocked mind.

'Kai! Look! The woman in white – Matilda!' she shouted, trying to make him turn back but he just walked relentlessly on towards the gate. She turned back and the presence had gone, if it was ever there in the first place. She caught him up and turned to him.

'Look, it's alright, I know you just come here to please me. I know you don't really believe in ghosts.'

He turned to her. 'I'm here, aren't I?' he said sadly. Bending forward, gave her the same feathery soft kiss on her cheek.

'Well, thanks for being here, Kai; I do appreciate it you know. See you next year?' she said hopefully, and he nodded. She looked in the direction of the train station. 'Will you be early for your train?'

'It doesn't matter' he said, 'I can always wait.'

'Do you mind if I leave you here then?' They had reached the gate and Ellie suddenly felt cold.

'No, of course not,' he smiled and she smiled back, then Kai turned and walked down the hill to the station.

Halfway down, the tears came, as they always did. He knew it was no good turning round for one more look as she'd have gone. Until the next time. 'Thanks for saving my life' she'd whispered to him – but he hadn't, had he? Hadn't managed to grasp her outstretched hand as she slipped and fell down the dungeon steps three years ago. At her funeral, he could hear her whispering in his ear. 'See you next year.' And it would be the same every year, as long as he could make it, because it was the only chance he would ever have of saving her life, even if it wasn't real. She slept there, not in the church graveyard where she was buried but in the Abbey ruins, where she died. Waiting every year to see him again. Seven-thirty at the Abbey.

Ghost in the Machine

by Peter Collins

Chloe James had been conned. The school brochure described Psychology as a fun and interesting subject, and she thought it would be a lot easier than Geography or German. But it turned out to be really hard. And even worse, she had Mrs Anderson as her teacher. Mrs Anderson was new to the school and she had Chloe marked out as trouble from the very start of term. Chloe could feel Mrs Anderson's eye on her now, even as she was giving the class their new assignment.

'Your project will be to write a piece on the theme of mind-body dualism,' intoned Mrs Anderson from the front of the class. 'Mind-body dualism concerns the consciousness of the human mind and how it relates to the physical body.'

She waved a DVD in her hand. She was a tall, angular woman and her movements struck Chloe as being needlessly aggressive.

'All the resources you require are on this disc. For the purposes of this assignment, you are not allowed to access any other materials. Once you have become familiar with the basic concept, you should then write your report. This will be a real test of your understanding of the concept.'

She distributed the DVDs, pausing only when she reached Chloe's desk. Chloe was a slightly built girl with straight dark hair. She looked an unlikely troublemaker, but Mrs Anderson knew better. She glanced over her shoulder and the door immediately opened to admit one of the Teaching Assistants who had been clearly waiting for her signal.

'You will do your work in the new Learning Centre, Chloe,' said Mrs Anderson deliberately. 'There will be fewer distractions for you there.'

Chloe opened her mouth to speak, but thought better of it. You couldn't win with some teachers. Reluctantly, she followed the TA to the newly-opened Learning Centre. Chloe had not been here before. It was a bright, airy space above the labs in the science block. The TA indicated a single desk with an old computer in the far corner of the room. The TA was a short, dumpy woman who wore a permanent expression of boredom like a facemask. She inserted a DVD into the computer.

'Everything you need is on the disk,' she explained in a flat monotone. 'That's all you can use. And don't think of trying the internet. The machine isn't connected to anything.' She turned and glumly made her way to a desk at the other side of the room.

Chloe sighed to herself and clicked on the DVD icon. Wording appeared on the screen.

Introduction to Psychology: Module 7

Mind Body Dualism: How consciousness arises in the brain.

Chloe frowned. She had no idea what the topic was about. She minimised the screen and searched for anything else installed on the computer just in case the TA had been wrong. There was nothing; no internet, no YouTube, no email. The only thing she could see was a small icon labelled *IMS*. She clicked it and a dialogue box appeared. It was nothing like the dialogue boxes that Chloe was used to seeing on her laptop at home. It had the words *Internal Messaging System* in an old-fashioned typeface at the top, and the background was an odd greenish colour. A full stop kept flashing in the box.

Chloe stared at it for a while. She looked up at the TA who was immersed in a Sudoku puzzle. Chloe shrugged. She reached for the keyboard and typed:

> \- *Does anybody know anything about Mind Body Dualism?*

She paused for a moment and then hit the return key. The message disappeared and the full stop started flashing again in the empty dialogue box. She stared at the screen, not sure what to expect. She waited a full minute and then another. Nothing happened. Chloe shrugged to herself and was just about to switch back to the DVD when the dot stopped flashing and a message appeared on the screen.

> - *Who's asking?*

Chloe blinked in surprise. Could this be Mrs Anderson setting a trap? Unlikely. Even so, she phrased her reply carefully.

> - *My name's Chloe. I'm doing some research for a project and I'd like to do well.*

Ha. Let's see Mrs Anderson tell her off for that! This time the reply came much quicker.

> - *Hi Chloe. My name's Oliver. I did that subject a few years ago. I can probably still remember most of it. Where are you by the way?*

Chloe knew enough about chat rooms to be wary of giving out too much personal information. She'd already given this total stranger her name. Did she want to give up her location? But it wasn't

like it was her home address or anything. And the
TA was still with her. She didn't see much risk.

> -   *I'm in the Learning Centre.*

She had barely finished typing when the reply was
on screen.

> -   *The Learning Centre? Where's
>   that?*

Chloe thought for a moment.

> -   *It's new. It used to be Room 17
>   over the science labs.*

Again, the reply came instantly.

> -   *That's a horrible room. Make sure
>   you open a window.*

> -   *It's all right. The windows are fine.
>   I think they've done it up a bit.*

The reply was on the screen almost as soon as
she'd finished typing.

> -   *Thank God for that. It used to give
>   me the creeps. Now, what do you
>   want to know about?*

Chloe began to type in details of her assignment.
They had three sessions over three days to
complete the piece. She had no idea where to start.
The next half hour passed in a blur. Oliver told her

about the views of different philosophers. He talked about the famous French thinker René Descartes. He began to explain the relationship between the mind and the body, and whether they could be separate entities. At first, Chloe didn't really get it.

- *But I don't see how the mind and body can be separate. We did this in biology. Its electro-chemical reactions in the nerve cells that cause thoughts, isn't it?*

She re-read her sentence after she'd posted it. She was hugely proud of herself. Perhaps she had been paying attention in class after all.

- *That's right in a way, but it's the brain that creates the reactions not the mind. It's a mechanical process. What about the Ghost in the Machine?*

- *What on earth does that mean?*

- *There was this philosopher called Gilbert Ryle. He talked about the mind working totally independently from the body. Imagine the body is a machine and the mind is working separately inside it. He called it "Ghost in the Machine".*

-	*So are you saying that the mind could still work even if it was separated from the body?*

-	*Well, I'm not sure that he ever said that, but think about it. Imagine if the mind could work even after it had been separated from the body. It probably wouldn't be able to work for long because it takes up too much energy, but imagine if it could.*

Chloe was really lost here, but Oliver was funny and patient. He explained more about the subject slowly and clearly. Almost for the first time in her life, Chloe found herself wanting to learn, so she was almost disappointed when the TA looked up from her puzzle book and called, 'Right, start finishing up, please.'

Chloe highlighted and copied all Oliver's text. She pasted the information into a blank document and saved it. Then she began to type in the dialogue box.

-	*Listen, Oliver. Thanks for all that. I have to go now.*

- *But that was fun. Can I talk to you again?*

- *Yeah. I'll be here again tomorrow. Will you be here?*

- *I'll try. Honestly, I'll try.*

Then the dialogue box closed and the screen went blank.

The following day, Mrs Anderson was slightly surprised to see Chloe arrive early for her lesson before impatiently urging the TA to take her to the Learning Centre. Once there, she waited for the TA to settle back with her Sudoku, before opening up the message box.

- *Hi, Oliver. Are you there?*

The response came straight away.

- *Is that Chloe?*

- *Yes it's me. How are you?*

- *Better now. I was worried you wouldn't be there.*

Chloe stared at the screen for a moment. She wasn't used to people worrying about her and she was surprised to discover it was a pleasant feeling.

The idea of being lonely at school was a new one for Chloe. She had a lot of friends, but they were mostly other kids like her who preferred to muck about at the back rather than listen to the teachers like the nerdy kids did. Perhaps Oliver was a bit of a nerd. He did know a lot of stuff. But he was helping Chloe, so nerd or not, she was on his side.

Oliver began to recap everything they had covered the day before to make sure that Chloe understood everything. To Chloe's surprise, she found that a lot of it had actually stuck. With Oliver's help, Chloe started to edit the information she had copied the day before. Oliver was funny and kind and Chloe found herself absently wondering what he looked like. It was one thing to be a bit of a nerd, but she hoped he wasn't an ugly nerd.

The end of the session came round far too soon and before Chloe realised the TA was once again telling her to finish writing.

- *Sorry Oliver. Got to go now.*

- *No. Please don't leave me.*

Although they were only words on a screen, there was something about them that made Chloe wonder. It was as if she could detect an air of desperation behind the words.

- *Don't worry, Oliver. I'll be back tomorrow.*

- *But I might not be able to come back.*

- *What do you mean? Tomorrow's a normal school day.*

- *It took a lot of effort to talk to you before and even more to be here today. Please don't go. Stay with me now or it might be too late.*

- *Oliver, I....*

The TA was almost upon her. Chloe had no choice but to stop typing and close the IMS screen with her message unfinished. She was aware of the TA looking suspiciously at her as she escorted her from the classroom.

For the rest of the day, Chloe found it harder than usual to concentrate on her schoolwork. There had been something disturbing about Oliver's words, as if he had been pleading with her. Chloe found it hard to shake off a feeling that he was in some sort of trouble.

The next day, Mrs Anderson was waiting in class. The TA and a bored looking IT technician were standing next to her.

'Come with me,' ordered Mrs Anderson curtly before Chloe could speak and all four of them marched off to the Learning Centre.

'We come down very heavily on cheating at this school, Chloe,' Mrs Anderson said sternly. She indicated to the TA at her side. 'Miss Parkinson tells me that yesterday she saw you accessing the internet or some sort of chat room. What have you been doing?'

'Just searching the DVD, miss,' Chloe said firmly. She'd been in this spot before and knew that the best option was never to admit anything.

The TA shook her head. 'No, Mrs Anderson, it certainly looked like she was doing something else?'

Mrs Anderson turned to the IT technician. 'Check this computer, please.'

But the technician stayed where he was.

'There's no point, Mrs Anderson. Look.' He indicated to the back of the PC. 'This PC's not on the network. It's not connected to anything.'

They followed his gaze. Unlike other PCs in the room, there were no wires connecting it to the cable box running along the wall.

'Check it anyway,' insisted Mrs Anderson. 'It might be wireless.

The technician shrugged and sat at the terminal. He hit a few keys and brought up a list of programs on the PC.

'Like I said. It's not connected to anything. No wireless, no internet, nothing.'

Chloe kept very still. She could see that the IMS icon had appeared on the screen. Unfortunately, Mrs Anderson had noticed it as well.

'Well, what's that then?'

The technician peered at it with interest.

'Blimey. I've not seen that in a while. That's the school's old internal messaging service. We've not used that in years.'

'Have you been messaging somebody for help, Chloe?' asked Mrs Anderson.

Chloe shook her head. 'No, miss.' But her voice wavered slightly.

Mrs Anderson frowned. She sat at the keyboard and started typing.

> \- *Hello. Can you tell me more about mind-body dualism?*

Chloe stared in horror at the screen. *Please don't answer*, she prayed. *Please*. The tension in the room had become quite palpable and the technician was looking strangely at both Mrs Anderson and Chloe.

'Mrs Anderson,' he said firmly. 'You're not listening to me. This machine is not connected to anything. That messaging system doesn't work. This must be the only machine in the school that's still got the old icon. It's simply not possible for anybody to respond.'

Mrs Anderson turned to Chloe. 'Well, it seems I must apologise to you,' she said grudgingly. She looked dangerously at the TA. 'I'll talk to you later.'

Chloe said nothing, but her mind was racing. Oliver must be smarter than she realised if he'd found some way to communicate using the old system.

The technician was still reminiscing about obsolete computers.

'That old messaging system was as basic as they come. We took it out years ago, about the time of the lab incident.'

The TA nodded in recollection, but Mrs Anderson looked puzzled.

'Before your time,' said the technician, 'there was an accident in the lab downstairs. Some chemicals were spilt and they gave off a toxic gas. The teacher got all the kids out in time, but nobody thought to look up here. One lad was in this room doing some revision and the gas poisoned him. They reckon he would have been OK if he'd had a window open.'

'Oh, it was terrible,' chipped in the TA quickly, keen to move conversation away from her earlier overzealousness. 'Poor Oliver died from the gas.'

Chloe's attention had started to wander, but the TA's words made her head jerk upwards.

'Did you say Oliver?' Chloe asked.

'That's right. Oliver Browning; smart lad.'

'He died here?'

'Yes. Right here in this room. It was shut up for a while. People didn't like coming in here. Some of the kids used to say it was haunted. It's only just been redone as a part of the new Learning Centre.'

Chloe's mind was in a whirl. From miles away she heard Mrs Anderson's voice.

'How tragic. What was the boy like?'

'Oliver? Nice kid. Very bright. You would have liked him Mrs Anderson; he was very keen on Psychology. But his real gift was Technology. He was an IT genius. It was like he knew how a computer felt. Some of the staff reckoned he could have been a teacher himself. Seemed like he had a way of getting other people to learn stuff.'

Mrs Anderson just nodded. She thanked the technician and told the TA to make sure that Chloe got on with her work. Then she headed back to her classroom. If she was embarrassed about accusing Chloe of cheating she showed no sign of it.

Chloe's fingers were trembling as she switched on the computer. She clicked the IMS icon and was typing as soon as the screen appeared.

-       *Oliver. Are you there? It's me, Chloe.*

There was no response. Urgently, she typed again.

-       *Oliver. It's OK. I know what happened with the accident. I know why you've been lonely.*

Still the screen stayed blank. Chloe tried one more time.

-       *Oliver. Please say something. I know it's hard, but please try. I won't leave you. I promise.*

But the screen did not change. Chloe sat back in her chair. A feeling of terrible sadness overwhelmed her. For a moment she almost felt like crying. After a while, she opened the document where she had saved her notes and began to type.

The next day, Chloe handed in her project along with the rest of the class. Mrs Anderson took all the scripts into the staff room and prepared herself for the chore of marking them over lunch. She sighed as she saw Chloe's work on the top of the pile. *Oh well*, she thought. *Better get this one out of the way first.* She took a sandwich from her lunchbox and absently began to read:

Ghost in the Machine

by

Chloe James

When I was first given this project, I thought that it made little sense. We know from the study of human biology that thoughts come from electro-chemical reactions in the nerve cells. The mind and body are intrinsically linked. But what if that was not always the case? What if somehow, the mind or the spirit of a person could be separated from their body? What if their spirit; their soul perhaps; could exist independently from the body even after the body had died? Wouldn't that soul feel isolated and alone? Desperate to make contact with somebody, anybody. So desperate that they would use all the skills they had possessed when they were alive in order to try to communicate from wherever they were. This is the story of one lost soul. A true ghost in the machine...

Mrs Anderson put down her sandwich and began to read in earnest.

The Man from No Man's Land
by John Pritchard
(2ⁿᵈ Place)

This account was collected during a trip to France, visiting a relative at the Trois Arbres cemetery. I talked to a farmer who had some interesting insights. We spoke of the 'iron harvest' of military debris that gets turned up by the ploughing every year. He mentioned that, at Verdun, the lightning still strikes vertically because there's so much metal in the ground. In a similar way, he went on, there are places on the old front line where, though the trenches are long gone, there are spirits still following their course across the fields.

I asked if he had encountered such spirits. He said he had not, but the local priest Father Jacques had told him privately of such an encounter. This concerned a revenant still seen in the area around dusk, some fifty years after the end of the Great War. It was often reported in the vicinity of the cemetery itself, as if visiting one of the graves, whether a comrade's or its own.

According to the farmer, Father Jacques decided to try and speak with it. He went to the cemetery, left a packet of cigarettes on the Stone of Remembrance, like an offering, and waited. Very late in the day, near dark, a figure came into the cemetery and approached the Stone. It took one of the cigarettes and smoked it in front of him, 'for all the world like Our Lord taking food when He appeared to the disciples after He had risen'. But Father Jacques had to strike the match himself, 'since the ghost told him its clothes had not been dry these fifty years or more.'

So they spoke to each other across the Stone, and this is what the spectre said to him. As to whether it found rest once it had shared its burden, the farmer said it had not been seen since then, but sometimes at twilight his dogs would start to bark for no good reason, and he always took care to get back home before the sun had set.

December 1914

They said it would all be over by Christmas. And they were right, it was – for some of us.

Take my mate, Dave Wheeler, for example. For him, the war ended on Christmas Eve. He raised his head an inch too far and a Jerry sniper shot him. I heard the sound the bullet made, like a rotten apple flung against a wall. The crack of the shot reached us a moment later, but Dave was halfway to the ground by then. By the time I turned around, he was as limp as a dropped sandbag. His eyes were open, watching me, but his brains were out and all over the trench.

I shouted his name and felt absurdly guilty that I'd missed the final moment of his life. His service cap lay at my feet, the khaki stained with crimson. They didn't give us helmets in those days.

He wasn't the first to fall, not by a long chalk. This had stopped feeling like a grand game months ago. The fighting had ground to a halt, but not the killing. We were face to face with the Kaiser's butchers and neither side would let the other pass.

So you'll forgive me if I didn't feel delighted when some of our lads, and theirs as well, decided they'd be friends for Christmas Day.

The previous night, just a few hours after one of them killed Dave, they were lighting candles in their trench and singing Silent Night, translating it into German as if to taunt us. A few of the lads sang back to them but most of us just wished we were at home.

The morning seemed unnaturally quiet. I waited for the first shells of the day to break the stillness into frosty fragments. But nothing happened. We smoked and waited.

'Merry Christmas!' someone called, in English, from the German trench.

'And to you too, Fritz!' one of our lot shouted. These exchanges continued for a time. Then one of the Jerries stood up slowly and waved at us with empty hands. I brought my rifle up.

'Easy, lad,' murmured Sergeant Baines behind me. I flexed my finger round the trigger, thinking we could make it one less Hun, but no-one else seemed in the mood to shoot him. After a while, some of our lads climbed cautiously over the parapet.

Jerry did the same and men on both sides ventured forward. Soon a group had gathered, khaki coats and grey mixed up in No Man's Land. I watched them exchanging smokes and souvenirs. I heard them laughing. Watching the German faces, I wondered which one of the bastards had shot Dave.

The Lieutenant didn't like it either, but he stayed in his dugout and pretended it wasn't happening. Sergeant Baines watched the meeting more indulgently. I took the opportunity to get out of the trench. It felt like climbing up out of a grave. I took off my cap and looked around. The countryside was ravaged, with craters gouged into the earth and trees chewed down to stumps. The day was cold, and the ground was frozen solid. I wondered if we'd still be here when summer came.

The truce lasted all day but, as dusk gathered, the men made their farewells and drifted back towards their lines. I climbed down to the firing step and picked my rifle up, not knowing when the war would start again. A few cigarettes glowed red in the chill twilight as the knots unravelled slowly and, it seemed, reluctantly. Some of the Jerries were clearly in no hurry. They were taunting us again, I realised, clinging to No Man's Land as we withdrew. I brought my rifle up and tucked the butt into my shoulder. A warning shot would send them on their way.

Some wore caps but others had those spiked, barbaric helmets. I focused on one who was staring at our line, maybe taking a last look at our defences. Like a marksman noting where the gaps might be.

Was this the man who had watched with stony patience yesterday, keeping his finger on the trigger till Dave raised his head into his rifle's sights?

He turned away towards his trench but insolently slowly. I studied him. My heart was beating hard. Even then, I was prepared to let him get to cover. If he hadn't dragged his feet, I would have let the bastard live.

I lined the sights up on him in the twilight. A part of me still willed the man to sense that I had drawn a bead on him. But he walked towards his trench with pure German arrogance. *All right*, I thought, *you've had your chance*. I squeezed the trigger, felt the rifle jolt and saw him fall like a collapsing scarecrow.

So ended the truce on our sector of the line.

Some of the lads took exception to that and wouldn't speak to me, even though I gave the bloke a chance, and we were all going to carry on where we left off. Even Sergeant Baines was disapproving. 'Since you like shooting Huns so much,' he said, 'you can do night stag until we get relieved.'

Standing sentry overnight is a soul-destroying business. In the wee small hours it gets so cold that not even the warmest coat can keep it out. You think you'll never sleep, and yet fatigue creeps up on you and the darkness thickens in your eyes. But you know you can't nod off because you're thirty yards away from men who want to cut your throat. And if you're found asleep on duty, you'll be shot.

So you can imagine that, as dusk fell the next evening, I wasn't looking forward to the hours ahead. I'd tried in vain to get some sleep in the darkness of a dugout, but the thump of Jerry's shells kept waking me. Yet the sector was still fairly quiet, or so the day watch told me. I drank some hot coffee and climbed the step to peer through a loophole in the parapet.

No Man's Land was indistinct in the fading, frosty twilight. Nothing stirred in the Jerry line, but I knew that they were wide awake as well. Though they wouldn't be able to see me in the dimness, a squall of bullets would seek me out if I so much as lit a cigarette.

Then, as I scanned the ground in front of me, I glimpsed a movement. A thrill of fear went through me and I brought my rifle up. It was surely too early for them to launch a trench raid. But then I saw the figure – not on hands and knees but up and stumbling. He was just a silhouette against the skyline, but I could clearly see his Hunnish helmet spike. He was moving slowly, as if he didn't realise that it wasn't dark yet and he was exposed. Something about his clumsy gait gave me an odd impression – not of a man trying to cross rough ground but a man who couldn't see.

I don't know why I thought it was the soldier that I'd shot, but suddenly I was convinced of it: that he'd lain out there since this time yesterday. Perhaps it was guilt and I wanted to tell myself I hadn't killed him, but at the same time I felt peeved that I had missed. Pulling the rifle butt into my shoulder, I settled my cheek against the wood and got him in my sights. Go on, I thought with irritation, get your bloody head down. But he seemed to be wandering aimlessly. I was surprised that no-one called out from his lines. If he deserved a second chance, it was wasted as I watched him. And if my first shot had put his lights out, then it might be a mercy to finish him right now.

Impatiently, I squeezed the rifle's trigger. For a moment I was dazzled by the flash. When my vision returned he'd disappeared. I drew back from the loophole just before a machine gun started up and bullets raked across the parapet.

'You're far too jumpy, Steadman,' Corporal Miller told me wryly as we listened to the rounds crack overhead. 'Just let the buggers get some kip and they'll lay off us as well.'

The machine gun's clatter stopped, and silence fell.

From then on it was an average night. The odd exchange of fire, and flares exploding now and then to bathe the ravaged earth in ghostly light. In between, it was pitch black. Long silences. Strange noises. When dawn welled slowly up at last, there was no one to be seen in No Man's Land.

I spent the next day trying to sleep and scribbling a letter to Nicole. She was the French barmaid I was courting, from a village inn behind the lines, well clear of this shambles. I wished I could be in her safe, warm bed right then.

I dozed off in the dugout and next minute I was there, lying on her feather mattress, running my fingers through her long fair hair. I don't know why I wrote to her: she didn't speak much English and I couldn't write it very well myself. But we didn't need words in any language when we were together. Her face was beautiful but grave, her wide eyes full of unspoken concern.

At length she raised herself and smiled sadly down at me. I knew she was going to put her dress back on and go downstairs to serve my fellow soldiers. As I lay admiring her for one last time, I glimpsed a stirring in the gloom behind her, as if someone else was with us in the room. A black, gnarled figure, reaching out to seize her even as she touched her finger to my lips.

I woke with a jolt, my body cold with sweat under my greatcoat. Two lads were talking in the trench, and someone else squished past through the thick mud. The light was grey beyond the canvas curtain. Still shaken, I emerged to get some air.

As we waited for the day watch to hand over, I took a look through the trench periscope as if I expected the ground between us and Jerry to look any different.

A shadowy figure in a spiked helmet loomed out of the lens.

'Christ, they're right on top of us!' I shouted, jumping up onto the firing step as I fumbled with my rifle's safety catch. I could see him through the gap between two sandbags – not as close as he'd appeared to be, but close enough and just outside our wire. My heart gave a fearful kick of recognition. It was him again, and yet it couldn't be. I got him in my sights and pulled the trigger. He lurched but didn't fall, although I surely hadn't missed him at that range. I worked the bolt and fired again at the dark shape in the twilight. He didn't topple even then, and I raised myself over the parapet to shoot once more, ejected the spent cartridge, and gave him a fourth bullet. Then the others grabbed my legs and dragged me back.

The Jerries gave our trench another pasting, while Corporal Miller yelled at me, demanding to know if I wanted to get killed. We waited, braced to fight off the attackers, but the hail of bullets petered out. Jackson took a look through the trench periscope and told us he could see nobody out there.

'Steadman, you're getting trigger-happy, man,' said Geordie Young.

That night was very cold, and it seemed endless. I'd never felt so jittery before. At one point I could have sworn I heard the barbed wire start to creak, as if some animal was caught in it and trying mindlessly to free itself. On and on it went, until my nerves were frayed to tatters. I urged the corporal to fire a flare and at last he did so just to shut me up. As the cold glow lit the night, I peered out between two sandbags but could see no movement in the tangled wire. The flare descended slowly, and the darkness flooded back.

I told myself it was just the rats I'd heard.

The next day I hardly slept, though I was groggy with fatigue. The horror couldn't be denied. The man I'd shot was coming after me. Every time I saw him, he was closer. I was increasingly convinced that tonight I would confront him in the trench. I already knew that bullets couldn't stop him. Perhaps it would take a bayonet. I might have to hack the heart out of his chest.

It didn't cross my mind to run, though the threat of a court martial was nothing compared to a man who wouldn't die. My mouth was dry with fear, of course. For what could be more frightening than the thought of a blind man in the darkness, seeking his revenge? But mostly I just felt resigned. I'd begun this thing between us. Now I had to make an end of it somehow.

As dusk came down, I listened to the stillness and gripped my rifle tight in sweaty hands. A look through the trench periscope had shown an empty landscape. Perhaps he was already in the trench with us, lurking somewhere along its crooked course, a spectre in the shadows.

I forced my finger off the trigger, in case I blasted one of my own blokes.

Then, in the last glimmer of the twilight, my gaze strayed to the field behind the trench. And there he was, ungainly as a scarecrow, a silhouette against the western sky. I froze stiff at the sight of him, but as I watched I realised he was stumbling away from us, as if he'd groped past blindly and gone on.

A wild relief washed over me – a sense of liberation. But then I felt my stomach start to sink. Beyond our support positions there was unprotected country, and this sightless thing was walking into it. If he couldn't get his hands on me, he might vent his wrath on others.

I suddenly thought he might know about Nicole.

Watching the shape recede into the darkness, I grew increasingly convinced that he would seek her out and claim her in my place. He was dead, after all, and yet he walked: what could be hidden from him? That dream of the shadow in her room had surely been a warning of some kind.

I looked around but no-one else was watching, so I slipped down the communication trench and followed it, heart pounding, till I reached the rear area. If I'd met someone, I would have told the truth – that I was following a Jerry infiltrator. But no-one was moving forward yet. The trench emerged into a sunken lane. It was almost dark, and the silence was unnerving. I went along the lane a little way till I glimpsed a movement up ahead and made out a dim figure, walking with a limping gait I recognised.

I followed him, keeping a wary distance. Behind me I heard the rumbling of guns like a storm on the horizon, coming from another sector. The countryside round here was deathly still.

Within a few minutes I lost him in the darkness and balked at the thought of going on. He might be lying in wait. The thought occurred to me that he could only move at twilight. At each successive dusk he had advanced only a dozen yards or so. Today he'd gone further, but then I hadn't tried to shoot him.

Tomorrow I'd have the chance to get ahead of him again.

I left the lane and managed to find shelter in a field barn, partly demolished by a shell. I didn't get much sleep. It wasn't just the gnawing cold but the noises in the darkness, as creatures which knew nothing of the war emerged from their holes and crept about. I huddled up and listened, drifting off to sleep from time to time, then waking with a start.

Just before dawn, I rejoined the lane and walked towards the village. The fields looked desolate, still grey with frost. Behind me the grumbling guns had fallen silent and I felt like the only soldier left alive.

The lane rose towards a little wood, the trees stripped bare by winter. I laboured up and, at the crest, I came across a wayside crucifix. I'm not a great one for church parade but something made me stop there. If I was going to confront a walking corpse, I would welcome any help that I could get.

I walked into the wood and hunkered down there, far enough in to see without being seen. The day might be short but it went by very slowly. I felt famished and exhausted but there was no going back. I'd deserted my post and left my mates. It could mean a firing squad. But that didn't matter. My only thought was how to save Nicole.

Very few people passed, because this section of the lane was on a forward slope and any movement might be seen. Now and again a runner scuttled down it. The distant guns kept booming fitfully.

Slowly the dusk came creeping in. A sick feeling grew inside me. My mouth was as dry as chalk again and I took a final swig from my canteen. No-one had passed for an hour or more. I moved to the wood's edge, unslung my rifle and prepared myself.

The shadows lengthened as the daylight faded. Gradually the empty lane was silted up with gloom. And then I saw him at the bottom, indistinct at first, like something stirring behind a dusty veil. Breathlessly I watched as he drew closer, lumbering awkwardly up the slope. I could make out the long coat and helmet spike. I half-raised my rifle and wondered, if I gave him all ten bullets, would they be enough to blow him back to Hell?

I knew this was my only chance to stop him. But how could I kill somebody twice? I'd already done my worst. When you've shot an unarmed soldier in the back on Christmas Day, whatever can you do to make amends?

Impulsively I stepped out of the treeline and stood before him in the lane. I held my rifle up in my right hand and threw it aside. It landed with a clatter and his head came up and turned towards the sound.

He was about ten feet away. I could just make out his features. The eyes were sunken, like black pits, no light in them at all. His livid face was slack and stood out palely in the twilight. For a moment he stood motionless, but I knew that he could sense me in his path. His empty gaze stayed on the fallen rifle but then he raised a hand and started pawing at the air as he took a slow step forward, then another. My heart quailed but I stood my ground. I couldn't have moved, even if I'd wanted to.

What could I say? *My friend, I am the enemy who killed you*? The thought lying behind that was barely formed:

Do what you will, but let my sweetheart live.

He showed his yellowed teeth as if to mock me, and shambled closer, reaching out. I stared into the hollows of his eyes, so fixated that I didn't hear the tramp of boots behind me, till a shout of warning broke the ghastly spell.

A rifle cracked and I felt a blow as if a horse had kicked me. It threw me towards the Jerry, but he disappeared before my staring eyes and I pitched onto the muddy road. More shots rang through the twilight. My body had gone completely numb. Face down in the mire, I found I couldn't breathe.

Footsteps approached but the voices sounded very far away.

Jesus, it's one of our own blokes.

He was fraternising with a Jerry, mun!

I don't see many Jerries round here, mate...

Their argument grew fainter. I tried with all my strength to crawl away, but my muscles wouldn't even twitch. The darkness thickened round me, and I felt myself drawn down into the earth.

*

I thought it was the end and I was grateful. Perhaps it was no more than I deserved. But instead of nothingness, there was a never-ending tunnel. And gradually it dawned on me that my punishment had only just begun.

When the tunnel opened up, it was still twilight. I found I was on my feet and walking, still in uniform, my rifle slung. I passed a group of soldiers by a hedgerow, smoking and talking nervously as they waited to move up to the front line. None so much as glanced at me, but they all lapsed into silence as if something had put a chill into their hearts.

I kept on going, following one path and then another. It was always dusk. The sun had gone but nightfall never came. Sometimes I passed men who never saw me. Others called out and began to shoot, but the rounds seemed as irrelevant as gnats.

The man I killed: he'd found his rest – and passed on his condition. Now I was the one left to roam the battlefield, an unknown soldier on patrol in a Hell of men's own making, condemned to a never-ending walk, across devastated fields, up half-known roads.

www.ingramcontent.com/pod-product-compliance
Lightning Source LLC
Chambersburg PA
CBHW032035180726
48284CB00008B/2595